"Call the police," I said. My voice was low and calm and sounded as if it were coming from someone else. I began to shiver, even though the evening was still warm. "We have to call the police."

"No, come on, help me get him to the car. We'll take him to the hospital."

Kirby had tried frantically to rouse Tigger—slapped him, shaken him, breathed into his mouth—and it hadn't done any good. I had tried both his neck and his wrist for a pulse. Nothing.

Kirby was struggling to lift the body, get him to his feet, but that wouldn't do any good, either.

"He's dead, Kirby," I said. "Leave him there, open the door and I'll call the police."

"Oh, God, no."

———————— ★ ————————

DEATH OF THE PARTY

Catherine Dain

WORLDWIDE.®

TORONTO • NEW YORK • LONDON
AMSTERDAM • PARIS • SYDNEY • HAMBURG
STOCKHOLM • ATHENS • TOKYO • MILAN
MADRID • WARSAW • BUDAPEST • AUCKLAND

DEATH OF THE PARTY

A Worldwide Mystery/March 2002

First published by Five Star.

ISBN 0-373-26415-1

Printed in U.S.A.

DEATH
OF THE
PARTY

ONE

"I KNOW I'VE SAID IT so often that you're probably
tired of hearing it, but it's still true. You need to move,
Faith," Michael said. He couldn't resist adding, "And
if you'd listened to me when I first said it, you
wouldn't have been robbed."

"Burglarized," I answered, annoyed at his smug-
ness. "You can only be robbed if you're there. If you
aren't in the house, and I wasn't, you've been burglarized. I suppose that never happens in West Hollywood."

"Not as much as it does in Silver Lake, especially
when you live south of Sunset. That was a charming
and convenient house when you were playing student,
but it isn't a good place for a professional. And besides,
the neighborhood has deteriorated around you. Six
years ago there wasn't anything like the kind of graffiti
you see now. I could visit you and park my car on the
street without wondering what it was going to look like
when I got back."

"I wasn't playing student. I don't see everything in
life as a role." I responded with the patience one would
expect from a licensed psychotherapist. "I was getting
an advanced degree in preparation for a serious career
change. My clients still think the house is charming.
And nothing has happened to your car. Mine was

sprayed once, I admit that, but it was three years ago, and it needed to be repainted anyway.''

''And three years ago we could have had lunch here without feeling we were in a prison yard.''

I had no answer for that. The patio of the tiny restaurant was almost entirely enclosed by a six-foot chain link fence.

The conversation wasn't making me feel any better. Michael had insisted on lunch when I had called that morning to tell him about the burglary the night before. He had even agreed to come to Silver Lake instead of arguing for West Hollywood, and I hadn't expected the heavy dose of I-told-you-so.

I picked up my coffee cup, so large it was almost a bowl, and drank the little bit of froth remaining. The caffe latte hadn't been quite hot to start with and now it was cold. At least the warm scallop salad had been good.

''I have a client at two,'' I said.

Michael reached across the table and took my hand.

''And Elizabeth has an appointment for her annual check up at two. But we're going to take the time. Tell me the whole story, all details,'' he said in his therapist tone, with an earnest therapeutic look in his eyes. ''You'll have to set the situation aside when your client comes, to focus on her, and telling it to me step-by-step first will help.''

''The client is male, actually. His wife sent him.'' I stopped myself from making a biting comment about what happens when therapists help therapists. ''He's my first male client, and I'm not totally comfortable with him under the best of circumstances. And you're right. I do need to talk a little more about the burglary first.''

"You aren't comfortable with your client because you aren't comfortable with men, and you haven't been since that professor left you for a younger student."

I glared at him. "I'm comfortable with male friends."

"How did you feel when you opened the door?" Michael asked, patting my hand.

"Disoriented." I shifted in the plastic chair, remembering. "It was my house, but it didn't look like my house. The stereo was gone. My jewelry box was sitting on the coffee table. I am compulsively neat, as you often remind me, and I don't leave things like that. I almost closed the jewelry box and put it away before it hit me that someone had been there. And then I felt violated."

"What an awful feeling," Michael said.

"Exactly." I couldn't help smiling. "Exactly what I would have said."

"Your gold jewelry was gone," Michael prompted.

"Yes. Only the gold, not the silver. Four chains, one pin—actually brass, a replica of a museum piece—and some earrings. My grandmother's engagement ring. The thief missed her cameo necklace and her pearl pin. I yelled for Norman and called the police while he unbarricaded himself. You think I should move. He just thinks I should get shutters and bars."

"I can't imagine that Norman and Helena have anything anyone would want."

"Helena's paintings of naked Normans with wings are sure to be collectible someday. Hairy angels will be in vogue sooner or later. And Norman was nice enough to sit with me—fully clothed—while I figured out what was gone and waited for the police."

"Did you feel the officer was helpful?"

"Well, she was nice, anyway. She didn't hold out much help that I would actually get anything back. We talked about whether I should get a gun."

"You don't want a gun."

Michael had interrupted at the same point the first time I had told him. We had never gotten back to the story. That was why I had been annoyed with him. This time I refused to be sidetracked.

"And then Marcus came in, because he had seen the black-and-white parked in front, and he wanted to make certain I was all right."

"I suppose he became an immediate suspect. Do you want another latte?" Michael was signaling the waitress.

"Yes. I hope this one isn't tepid. And no, Marcus wasn't a suspect. Although he explained why my closet was messed up and why my computer wasn't taken."

"Why?"

"People store drugs in shoe boxes and computers have no street value. Officer Magnum said he was right."

"That wasn't her name."

"Yes, it was. And she's used to the jokes. She was tough and professional, too. Clint Eastwood's last girl friend, what's her name, could play her in the TV movie."

"You're thinking of a comeback as yourself?"

"No." Actually, the thought had crossed my mind, but I had dismissed it. "Anyway, Norman hissed at Marcus because his music is so loud, and Marcus told him to chill out. Officer Magnum told me not to touch anything until the fingerprint man came. She wasn't interested in the blood."

"What blood?"

"The burglar got in by breaking one of the bedroom windows with a rock." I permitted myself a little satisfaction from Michael's surprise. "He cut his finger when he reached in to open it. Officer Magnum said blood type wouldn't help catch him, and there wasn't enough for any kind of DNA test. She was amused that I asked. Norman asked if he could replace my deadbolt, and she said yes. It seems the thief had gone out the front door, taking my spare keys with him."

"How did he find them?"

"Everyone but me seemed to think that under the fruit bowl in the kitchen was an obvious place to look."

The waitress, a young Latina with long hair and gold earrings that dangled halfway to her shoulders, arrived with two more large, round cups of latte.

"You can bring the check," Michael told her.

I took a sip of the latte. It was warmer than the first, but the milk hadn't been steamed quite long enough, that was the problem.

"Officer Magnum thinks we should form a Neighborhood Watch."

"She thought that gallery of grotesques living on your block should do something communally? Weren't Norman and Marcus enough to convince her otherwise?"

"Marcus had left and Norman was working on the deadbolt. And I think it might be a good idea. I didn't have time this morning, but I'll try to talk to Alex this afternoon, to see if we can hold it in his living room."

"A black musician, a white bigot with an artistically challenged wife, two gay guys who are into S and M, and you. Good luck."

"How do you know Alex and Wayne have a sado-masochistic relationship?" I asked, perking up.

Michael gave me a glance that might have been withering if I couldn't have excused the question as professional curiosity.

"Alex is pierced and tattooed. Wayne isn't. Wayne works. Alex sits at home and drinks. I could be wrong."

"I'll have to observe more closely," I said. "Listen for screams."

"Haven't you heard of gags?"

"Oh." I'd heard of them. I just hadn't thought of them. "And there are other people on the block, the Hispanics across the street, for example, the ones with the 'Republic of Cuba in Exile' bumper sticker. I don't know who they are. And there's Christopher, who lives upstairs from Wayne and Alex."

"Another Illustrated Man. He'll help, I'm sure."

"He might. Besides, at least I'll feel as if I'm doing something useful. And I promised Officer Magnum I'd try to set up a meeting."

"Moving would be doing something useful."

"I know you think that. But moving right now would feel like running away, and I just don't want to do that. I want to reclaim my space first. When I move, whenever I move, I want to be moving to, not moving from."

"Anywhere you move is moving to," Michael began, then stopped. "All right. But how can you stay there? Aren't you afraid? Even a little?"

"A little," I admitted. "But I can handle it. Besides, Amy and Mac are there, and they think of it as home. They love the backyard."

"And they're cats."

"Elizabeth is a cat. You arrange your life around her."

"Elizabeth supports me. Or Pretty Kitty cat food supports me, however you want to look at it. But you're right. I do take her into consideration, and I would even if she weren't a television star. Nevertheless, I think Amy and Mac would handle a move just fine."

"Norman replaced the deadbolt last night, and my landlord arrived this morning with a new pane of glass for the bedroom window. The fingerprint man spread black powder around, getting one partial that might be useful, and I cleaned up the mess after he left. Everything back to normal. I'm looking forward to going home and resuming my life. I'm not ready to move."

"Okay." Michael pulled out his wallet and picked up the check.

"How much?" I asked.

"This one's on me. Only because you'll have to replace the jewelry and the stereo."

"And whatever is missing from my closet."

"What?"

"I don't know what it is. I just look in there, and it doesn't seem right. I think he took something. I'll look again later, check again. And thank you for lunch."

"You're welcome. Are you ready to listen to your client?" Michael was standing, wallet and check in hand, preparing to leave.

"Yes. Thank you for that, too."

"Let me know what happens with the Neighborhood Watch." He kissed my cheek.

I watched him go inside to pay. His round face, thin body, blue jeans, and general liveliness made him seem younger than I knew he was. Only a few gray hairs marked him as possibly close to forty. He was in fact forty-one, two years older than I. We had been friends for years, since he had come to the cast party of a play I had starred in. One of the highlights of my acting career. One of the few.

Being a therapist was better. And my client was expecting me.

The restaurant was only half a mile from my house. I could have walked, but the walk home would have been mostly uphill. And I hadn't been exercising much, which accounted for the fact that I had gained fifteen pounds since I left graduate school and started working at home.

Michael didn't come back to the patio. I remembered that he had to take Elizabeth to the vet. They would probably be late because he had stayed to listen to me. And I did appreciate his friendship.

I picked up my black leather bag and left through the gate in the chain link fence. I had parked the blue Taurus in front of the art gallery—or at least the storefront travel agency that displayed local artists—next door. The sun was shining, the sky was clear, and it was all-in-all a near-perfect April day.

If I moved, I would miss the neighborhood.

I drove the few blocks home, got out of my car to open the garage door, and stopped.

Norman was applying fresh paint over fresh graffiti.

"That's really nice of you," I said, not quite looking at him. I couldn't help remembering that underneath the plaid shirt and torn jeans was the hirsute pink body that Helena, his wife, had decided was the perfect decoration for their living room walls. Several times over.

"I had to paint mine," Norman said. "I might as well paint yours. If I don't, it'll just get worse."

"Officer Magnum thinks we ought to start a Neighborhood Watch. Are you interested?"

Norman stopped painting and glared.

"That depends on who's coming," he said.

"Everyone will be invited," I said firmly.

Norman went back to work without commenting. He had been down to the last corner when I arrived.

He picked up the paint can and pulled the door handle up, exposing the empty garage. I had stopped storing anything but my car in there after the first time it was broken into.

"I'll close it after you," he said. "No sense both of us getting paint on our clothes."

I drove the car into the garage and got out. He pulled the door shut and locked it behind me.

"Thank you. I'll let you know about the meeting."

Norman shook his head and went up the stairs next to mine. The two houses were almost side by side on the lot, owned by the same person, with mine slightly farther back—thus higher—from the street. It was a Southern California stucco bungalow, complete with red tile roof, probably built in the thirties. The current owner had painted it an improbable Wedgwood blue that still made me wince occasionally.

Once inside, though, I could forgive the color of the outside. There was too much else to love, like the refinished hardwood floors in the living room and dining room, and the airy kitchen, and the way the wisteria almost covered my bedroom windows.

Turning the dining room into an office meant that the only place to eat was now a tiny breakfast nook, but that was a minor disadvantage. The blank space in the living room where my stereo had been was more serious.

I was still wondering what to do about it when my client arrived—Jack Griffin, the man pushed into coming by his wife Linda, whose best friend was also my client. It cheered me to realize that I was starting to get referrals. And I would certainly become more comfortable having male clients after the first.

I ushered him smoothly into the dining room office, so smoothly that he didn't notice the missing stereo, and seated him in the comfortable green armchair.

"So how was your week?" I asked, taking my own place in an authoritative leather chair across from him.

"Awful, Faith. We were burglarized."

I bit my lip.

"Some bastard broke a window to get in," Jack continued. "It's enough to make you crazy."

"It certainly is," I murmured supportively.

Jack's story was even longer than my own, including his reactions and Linda's as well. After the broken window, the coincidences stopped. And the end of the story led him back to his relationship with Linda.

"She just won't listen to me," he said. "Women are supposed to be like you—they're supposed to be caretakers, nurturers, listeners. Not like Linda. Always wanting her need to be met. I don't give a shit about her needs."

"I'm paid to listen," I reminded him. "This is a professional relationship."

"What are you saying? That I should pay my wife to listen to me?"

"No. I'm pointing out that there are different kinds of relationships, formed for different purposes. Each of you—you and Linda—seems to feel ignored by the other in some fundamental way. Maybe you could offer her an exchange of time. She listens to you for fifteen minutes, then you listen to her. And you both agree to listen without judging.''

"I'll think about it."

"Good. And you can let me know next week if it works. For now, our time is up."

I stood, taking what I hoped was an authoritative stance. Jack Griffin was a bulky man, sweating in his white shirt and loose tie, and I was careful not to appear intimidated as I moved toward the front door, hoping he would follow. I could hear him ease himself out of the chair. When I turned, he was right next to me.

"Next week," he said smiling.

I had barely shut the door behind him when Amy appeared in the archway to the abbreviated hall that connected living room, bedroom, kitchen, and bath. Amy was a long-haired sable cat with a huge tail, originally part of a litter born to a neighbor who had since moved. Mac trotted up behind her. Mac, still Amy's baby even though the cats were five and six, looked so much like her that I suspected an incestuous relationship between Amy and the massive tom who had fathered her. Nothing had been added to the gene pool.

Amy didn't like Jack, so she avoided the front of the house during his sessions. And whatever Amy did, Mac did as well.

"You may be right about him," I said to Amy. "I wonder sometimes if I should start giving clients one of those personality inventories before I take them on. I am not equipped, emotionally or intellectually, to handle anything more than a garden-variety neurotic."

Amy blinked, then hopped onto a sofa covered in a rough, sand-colored material. Mac hopped up after her. She leaned against a fringed blue throw pillow to give him a bath. I was slowly getting rid of the Southwestern look, but some pieces remained.

"I'll be back soon," I told them.

Jack Griffin had left me tired, but I wanted to get started on the Neighborhood Watch, and I had a client coming at five, prime time for psychotherapists. Jack came in earlier because he was a real estate agent who could set his own hours.

I cut through Norman and Helena's gazania to get to the two-story duplex on the other side, a mustard stucco with curling vines of orange and magenta bougainvillaea. Alex and Wayne lived on one side. Their friend Christopher lived on the other.

"Come in, Faith darling," Alex said, smiling, scratching his curly blond beard. His face was lined, skin starting to sag, but I wasn't sure whether it was because of age or dissipation.

"Did I get you up?"

"No, no. Come on in and get yourself some coffee. I'll just take a minute to get some clothes on."

Alex was wearing a silky brown robe that came just to his knees, exposing the tail of a red and green dragon on his shin. The head of that or another dragon peered over the vee of the lapels on his chest, and one small complete dragon coiled around his left forearm. What skin showed around the tattoos had the unhealthy pallor that came from little attention to diet and no sunshine.

When I first met Alex, I had been disconcerted by the tattooes and the three small earrings, two studs and a hoop, that Alex wore in his left ear. But I didn't much notice them after the first year.

I waited in the living room while Alex went upstairs to the bedroom to get his clothes. A muted Geraldo was watching two people shout at each other on the large television screen. Below the television set on the oak entertainment center was an empty space where a VCR had been two weeks before. I had seen a young man going over the back fence with a VCR under his arm, but by the time the police had arrived, the young man was long gone.

The room reeked of stale cigarettes. A large ceramic ashtray on the heavy oak coffee table was overflowing. My nose twitched, and I stifled a sneeze.

I wanted to peek at the current issue of *Hunk,* which was on the coffee table next to the ashtray, but I would have been embarrassed if Alex had caught me. I sat down in a small, round chair to watch Geraldo gesture at his audience.

Alex returned wearing jeans and a white T-shirt that revealed a portion of yet another dragon, this one on his right bicep.

"Are you sure you don't want coffee?" he asked. "I'll get you some."

"No, I'm not going to stay long. I have a client coming."

Alex looked at me expectantly, through wide brown eyes with thin tired lines around them.

"I was burglarized sometime yesterday," I said, as flatly as I could. "I discovered it when I got home from the clinic last night. And I think we ought to form a Neighborhood Watch."

Alex shrugged his narrow shoulders.

"What makes you think it would do any good?"

"Well, I saw the guy who took your VCR go over the fence when he was leaving. Maybe somebody saw him arrive, but didn't want to interfere. And maybe if everybody knew Tuesday and Thursday are the days I go to the clinic—the two days I'm not here seeing clients—somebody would have noticed the burglar heading in or out. And everybody would know that strangers hurling rocks at windows are all of our business.''

"I'm not hopeful." The tired lines around his eyes meant Alex never looked hopeful. I was sorry to hear he didn't feel that way, either. "When the burglar broke in here, I was only gone for a few minutes, to the grocery store, and I'm not going to call you, or anybody, every time I go out. But if you want to organize it, I'll come."

"Good. Can we hold the meeting here?"

"Why?"

"Your living room is larger and closer to the street." And I didn't want people smoking in my house, but I didn't feel like antagonizing Alex by reminding him of that. "What night would be good for you and Wayne?"

"I'll have to check with Wayne, but I think Tuesday would be fine."

"Let me know for sure and I'll coordinate it with the community relations person at Rampart."

"And you'll invite the block."

"Yes."

Alex shrugged again and reached for a cigarette.

I took that as my cue to leave.

I cut back through Norman's yard and crossed my own to get to the white frame house on the other side. I knocked on the kitchen door.

Marcus took so long to answer that I almost gave up.

"Hey, baby, what's happening?" Marcus smiled, a sleepy smile, showing very white teeth. His face was dominated by that mouth and the fringe of hair and moustache that framed it. He looked as if he ought to be a singer. In fact, he played the piano. Marcus was wearing gray sweat pants. Only. If he had any tattoos, they were in very private places.

"I got you up. I'm sorry. I just wanted to thank you for coming over yesterday." I could feel my face turning red. I backed down a step.

"No problem. I gotta be up late tonight, got a few friends coming over, and I wanted to get some sleep first. Listen, why don't you stop by? Have a glass of wine, hear a little music, enjoy the party?"

"Thanks. Maybe I will. And is Tuesday okay with you for a Neighborhood Watch meeting? The officer suggested we form one, and I think it's a good idea."

"It is a good idea. I didn't mention it before, but there are strange things happening on this block. Someone knocked on the front door a few nights ago, three o'clock in the morning, to ask directions to Pasadena."

"Asking directions at three a.m.? And if he was on the way to Pasadena, how did he get to this block?"

"I don't know nothing about it. Ask Louie—he answered the door. You know, I used to live in a really bad neighborhood. But if somebody got shot down the street, that was a private affair. Now I've moved up to the middle class, and people bar their doors and windows because they're getting ripped off." He shook a sleepy head.

"Neighborhood Watch," I said firmly.

"Sure, girl. But remind me, will you? I gotta go back to bed now. Gimme a kiss." He held out his cheek.

I pecked the air. "I am an adult female, and that makes me a woman. How would you feel if I called you boy?"

Marcus grabbed me and hugged me. "Depends on how you mean it. No offense meant, none taken."

I struggled for a moment, then hugged back. After all, Marcus was a friend.

"See you at the party."

TWO

"Fay! For god's sake, Fay!"

I froze, plate of food in one hand, glass of wine in the other. The name was from my recent past, but the voice was one I hadn't heard in years. At least not live. And I rarely played his tapes anymore.

Going to Marcus's party had seemed a good idea when he asked, but it had become less attractive once my last client left. I had been tired—listening to a memory of childhood sexual molestation had exhausted me, in fact—and I didn't know any of Marcus's friends. Or I hadn't thought I did.

Once people had started to arrive, though, and I realized how big the party was going to be, I decided it would be better to attend the party than to spend the evening next door to it. I hoped he had invited neighbors in all directions, including Norman and Helena.

What to wear was a problem. The crowd trooping up the steps sported the gamut, torn jeans to silk and velvet. My gold jewelry was gone, and anything tight was out. I could live with my weight gain, but I couldn't flaunt it. I ended up choosing a purple scoop neck top and pants, cotton, cut with a loose drape. Silver belt and earrings.

For the second time that day, I cut across the yard to Marcus's kitchen door.

"You are HOT!" Louie screamed when he opened
it. "Purple! I love it!"

Louie was Marcus's roommate, after a fashion. He
had no visible means of support, other than whipping
up occasional costumes for friends, and his principal
tasks seemed to be keeping an eye on several thousand
dollars worth of electronic equipment in the back bedroom and feeding Marcus's three Siamese cats while
Marcus was on tour. This evening he was wearing one
of his own creations, a snakeskin and black velvet
sweatshirt over black leather pants. He had a three-day
growth of beard, and a long black pigtail curved around
his shoulder.

"The snakeskin was an inspired choice," I said.

"Do you love it?"

"Absolutely."

"I heard about the burglary," Louie said. "I'm glad
you're all right."

"I'm fine. Marcus said somebody strange had
knocked on your door a few nights ago. Did you call
the cops?"

"No. I will tomorrow." Louie glanced over his
shoulder. The kitchen was filling up with people.
"Come in and party. I'm glad you're not upset."

"That's not true—I am upset about the burglary. I
think we need to form a Neighborhood Watch."

He stopped to look at me. "Do you really want to
punish whoever did it? It was probably just a kid, you
know. Somebody grabbed my bag on the street once,
I just let him go. Figured he needed it more than I did."

"Yes," I snapped. "I want to punish whoever did
it, even if it was just a kid. If he had taken my computer, with all my notes and records, I'd want him mu-

tilated and branded. I might even be willing to do it myself.''

Louie stepped back, looking so startled at my vehemence that I almost relented.

''Let me get you some wine,'' he said. ''And introduce you to Denise. She did all the food.''

There's a look some women have that says they've spent all of their short lives being walked over by men. Sometime I'm going to write an article about it. Nicole Brown Simpson had it, and so did some of the women who came to the clinic. It was something in the eyes, begging for love and fearing a blow. Something about the mouth, the smile that was a little too eager. Denise had that look.

She was pale, skin and hair, too young to be that washed out. The makeup on her lips, cheeks, and eyes was an attempt at colorful that veered to harsh. She was wearing a dress that looked like lingerie, showing bones with so little flesh covering them that it was hard to imagine her doing the food. There was a faded bruise on one thin shoulder. I hoped Marcus hadn't put it there, or at least not intentionally.

When Denise smiled, a frightened, eager smile, I smiled back.

I liked Marcus and wished he were seeing somebody other than Denise. Because if he did treat her well, she would probably leave him for someone who wouldn't. I wanted to give Denise my card. Therapy would help.

Denise pointed me toward a buffet table full of cold-cut platters and salads and fruit and desserts. I put small spoonfuls of potato salad and pasta on my plate, then piled it with greens, unhappily conscious of how heavy I looked standing next to Denise.

I had just turned away from the table, reminding

myself that skeletal thinness was not healthy, uncertain what to do next, when I heard the voice. The deep, rich, full, mellow, heart-stopping voice.

"Fay! For God's sake, Fay!"

I turned around, and there he was, smiling at me, laughing that same high chuckle, incongruous next to the timbre of his low musical voice. His swept-back brown hair was a little thinner, there was a little gray in his brown beard. He had grown the beard in college to hide his round cheeks. His eyes were brown and eager, unchanged in almost fifteen years.

"Kirby." I had trouble finding the word.

"Fay, how are you? You look terrific."

"You, too."

He was dressed conservatively for this group, a gray jacket over a blue polo shirt and slacks. Something he might have worn in college. Still.

"God, it's good to see you!" he said.

"You, too." I didn't know what else to say to him.

"What's happened to you? You were on that soap, and then on the morning television show, and then you disappeared."

"The show was cancelled, and so was I. I had to find another career."

Kirby shook his head. "I loved to watch you in the mornings. I'd flick on the television, and there you were, a big star."

"You're the star. You have been ever since you played that renegade Texan in *Vietnam Brigade*." My smile was getting tight. This was embarrassing, making small talk with Kirby.

Someone wearing artfully arranged silk strips bumped my arm, almost spilling my wine.

"You have a full plate," Kirby said, "and I'm standing here like a fool with an empty glass. Let me get a refill, and then let's sit down somewhere quiet—if there is any place quiet—and talk."

"How about the back porch?"

Kirby nodded. "I'll be there."

I threaded my way back through the crowd in the kitchen and out the door. I sat down on the step, not really certain Kirby would follow.

But he did.

"You're not eating?" I asked.

"I have to watch my weight. If I don't, I look like Orson Welles."

"You do a little, don't you? It's the cheeks."

"Don't." Kirby sniffed—that funny sniff people who have just snorted cocaine sniff, with thumb and forefinger on their nostrils so they won't lose anything. He rubbed his fingers on his gums and took a sip of his drink.

I started to comment and stopped myself. This was a party. Most of the guests were probably doing something more than wine. We lived in the recreational drug capital of the world. And at least Kirby wouldn't have to steal to buy it.

"Orson Welles was handsome when he was young," was all I said.

He frowned at me, then softened. "What are you doing now? Tell me about your life. I miss you in the mornings."

"I was only on for four months. And that was five years ago. The program bombed so badly that no one would hire me afterwards. So I went back to school and got another degree and changed my name. I'm Faith, now."

"Faith? I liked the name Fay Cassidy. Why did you change it?"

"Fay Cassidy was an actress. Faith Cassidy is a therapist."

He cackled. "An actress playing a therapist. I know you."

"You knew me," I corrected. "I've grown up. And I'm sure you have, too."

"Is that how you see it?" He took another sip of his drink, then studied the glass as if there were a vision in the ice. "I have an idea for a movie. It opens with an establishing shot of a big house at night, in a storm, with thunder and lightning booming and crackling, tree limbs crashing down, just missing the roof. The camera zooms in on a second story window, the only one with a light. Inside the room a woman is sitting, reading. She's beautiful, in an original way, beautiful because she's her own person. She has lustrous hair curling around her shoulders, the color of autumn leaves streaked with gold, a hint of gray at the roots. Dark eyes, just starting to show faint lines at the corners. A firm chin, and cheekbones that will carry her into old age."

I wanted to tell him I didn't dye my hair, I just added highlights, but I didn't want to interrupt. I also didn't want to think that growing up meant looking older. And getting heavier.

"The storm is distracting her," Kirby continued. "She's restless, she can't read any longer. She puts the book down. A great clap of thunder, with lightning so close it almost hits the house, draws her to the window. A man is standing there, in the tree. She opens the window. He walks in. He's dressed all in green, except for the wet, scraggly feather in his cap, even green boots. His beard is gray. He's soaked from the rain. 'Hello, Wendy,' he says to her. 'Peter,' she says, 'you've grown up.'"

He was looking wildly around the yard as he finished. I thought for a moment that he was going to spring up and walk away. Then he started to cackle again, the moment of madness passing from his brown eyes.

"The movie is a comedy, by the way." He took another sip of his drink. "I'd rather call you Fay."

"Okay. No Faith."

He glanced at me and shook his head. "Tell me why you left television. I meant it when I said I missed you. Seeing your face would soothe my angry soul. I was depressed for a month when you left *Saints and Sinners,* and then I found you on that talk show. I'd turn on the set and there you'd be, interviewing some asshole who'd written a book, never losing your smile, and I'd think, 'There's Fay, who's practically a saint herself, and she's doing all right.'"

"Not a saint at all. I just played one on television. It's too bad you weren't a Nielsen family, or twelve of them. And a postcard wouldn't have hurt."

"I thought about calling, I really did. I didn't know where you were."

"And you couldn't remember my last name, so you couldn't look me up in the telephone directory."

"The phone book? Are you in the phone book? Oh, Jesus, I was sure you were unlisted. I never checked."

I thought of all the ways he could have found me if he had wanted to. The TV station, SAG, AFTRA, old friends.

"Kirby, I left television because nobody wanted to hire me. Really. I left *Saints and Sinners* because the producers killed me off. The daytime talk audiences only validated their opinion." I picked at the food. "I tried to get some attention doing local theater. Nothing happened. I was only thirty-four, and I was already hearing that I was too old and not pretty enough. That I'd had my shot at success and didn't make it. Not deferential to men was probably said behind my back."

"You?" Kirby widened his eyes in shock.

I ignored him. "I dropped out for a couple of years and went to graduate school. I have a license to practice as a psychotherapist and a new career. Are you sure you don't want some food? I took more than I want."

"No, thanks."

I put the plate down, uncomfortably aware one more time of the weight I had gained since I left television.

"What about you?" I asked.

"A couple of movies that did all right, a couple of CDs that didn't."

"Other than your career. The last I heard you were married to Tara O'Brien."

"Tara is gone with the wind," he announced formally.

"How many times have you said that?"

"A lot. She left me two years ago. It was a messy divorce. I'm surprised you didn't hear."

"I guess it didn't make the cover of the *National Enquirer*. Do you want to tell me about it?"

"No."

"Oh. Well, where are you living now?"

"That's one of the good things that's happened. I'm back in the old neighborhood again. I live about two miles from here. You can almost see my house from Marcus's front yard."

"Here?" I asked. "You're living in Silver Lake?"

"Actually Los Feliz, but I'm close."

"Why is this the old neighborhood?"

"Didn't you know I grew up here? Went to Madison High?"

"I did know. I'd forgotten."

"Where do you live?"

"There." I pointed at the house.

"There? There?" Kirby started to chuckle, a sound that rose higher and higher until he was almost silent, just shaking his shoulder. "Well, my stars, little darling, fate certainly brought us together again."

He threw an arm around me and planted a wet kiss on my cheek. His beard tickled. I had forgotten how soft his beard was.

"You feel good, Fay," he whispered. "I've missed you."

"I've missed you sometimes. Sometimes I haven't."

I looked at his eyes, red-rimmed and fierce. He blinked, and for a moment I felt sorry for him. I kissed his cheek.

"Hmmm," he said. "You can do better than that."

"Kirby, it's been fifteen years, it didn't exactly end well, and what do you want from me?" I snapped.

"You're right. I'm a clod. 'It's been fifteen years, and it didn't exactly end well,'" he mimicked. "I don't know what I want, except to embrace your body and feel your arms around me. I want what I had with you."

"Well, it's gone. Long gone."

"You're still mad."

"No, I'm not still mad." I sounded angry, even to myself. I worked to soften my tone. "I can't sustain any emotion for fifteen years, certainly not anger. But it's a long way from not being angry to wanting to start again. Or were you thinking in terms of a one-night stand?''

He glared at me. ''You used to have a sense of romance and adventure, you know.''

''And I'd like to think I still do. But the thought of going to bed with you doesn't feel romantic or adventurous. It's more like returning to the scene of the crime. Self-destructive, I think is the word.''

''Ha! You see yourself as perpetrator, then, not victim!'' He did his funny sniff again and shifted away from me restlessly.

I wondered how much cocaine he had, in him or on him. And whether he would offer me any. And what I would do if he did. I took a deep breath, thinking how long it had been since I had been high. I had developed a little bit of a cocaine habit—that was all it was, a habit, not an addiction—when I had been doing that morning television show, *Coffee Break*. I had needed it then, needed it to be up and perky for the assholes who had written books. My nose twitched, remembering. Not a good idea to think about it now.

''Victim has become a dirty word in our society,'' I said. ''I don't see either of us as perpetrators or victims. We were both participants. Nevertheless, sometimes I think what happened may have been a crime of sorts. I did love you, you know that.''

''I know. And I was too callow to love you as you should have been loved.''

''I was too unsure of my own identity to accept it if you had.''

I was starting to enjoy being with him, not certain if I wanted to give in to the feeling. Talking with him felt a little like dancing. I had to be careful, or sleeping with him might indeed seem like an adventure.

"Hey, man, are you here to play or to sit out on the porch here with my neighbor?" Marcus was standing behind us in the doorway. He winked when I turned, startled. "Not that I blame you."

"In a minute," Kirby boomed. "I'll be there in a minute."

Marcus disappeared into the kitchen.

"How can you and Marcus play together? You play mainstream rock with a country influence, his roots are rhythm and blues."

"But we were both influenced by the black folk who influenced Elvis."

"Jesus, that's condescending. What would Marcus say if he heard you?"

"He'd laugh. Fay, I want to see you again. Soon. Tomorrow."

"Not tomorrow. It's Saturday, I have clients most of the day. And I need to think about this. Call me Monday."

"I'll call you Monday and ask if you want to go to the beach. What do you think about a picnic lunch on the beach?"

"Call me Monday. And I don't have clients on Wednesday. I take Sunday and Wednesday off." I picked up my plate and stood.

Kirby rattled the ice in his empty glass.

"Time to play," he said.

I followed him into the kitchen. He was big enough, broad-shouldered and imposing, so that people moved to let him through. I left the plate on top of a stack next to the sink, making certain that Denise wasn't around to see how much food I was wasting.

The kitchen was hot and noisy, and the dining room

was worse. I wasn't certain I wanted to stay, even to hear Kirby and Marcus jam.

Kirby disappeared toward the bathroom. That meant he wasn't going to offer me any of his blow. He came out a few seconds later looking as if Tinker Bell had sprinkled fairy dust on him.

"Marcus!" he roared. "Let's do it!"

The crowd became quiet, silence spreading in ripples, but Kirby's voice wasn't the stone. Someone had opened the front door. Two uniformed policemen stood there.

My immediate thought was that Norman had called the police because of the noise. I sniffed for marijuana, hoping any use had been confined to the back bedroom. As the guests backed away from the door, I moved forward.

"And since the body was so near the front of this house, we thought you might be able to help us out," one of the officers was saying to Marcus. "We'd like an identification, if possible."

"What body?" I asked.

"There's a dead body in the street, ma'am," the officer said. "Do you live here?"

"Next door. Was it hit and run?"

"No, ma'am."

"And someone called you about the body?"

"We were responding to a call about the noise at the party here when we spotted what turned out to be a corpse."

"No more noise," Marcus said. He didn't need to raise his voice. The room had been clearing behind him, guests slipping out through the back door. "Let's see who the man is."

Marcus followed the police officers, and I followed Marcus. Kirby fell into step next to me.

The corpse was illuminated by the streetlight and the headlights from three cars. Someone was taking pictures, the flash periodically whiting out the scene.

The two officers ushered us through the temporary cordon so that we could view the body—a young Hispanic, lying on his back, not blinking at the lights. Blood suffused the front of his white T-shirt, his blue jeans, and his jacket.

I didn't know the young man. But I knew the black silk bomber jacket he was wearing. And then I realized what had been missing from my closet.

THREE

"WATCHING FOR BURGLARS is one thing. Watching for murderers is something else altogether," Michael said when I called him the next morning. "You can't go on with this."

"Can't form a Neighborhood Watch? Of course we can. It's more important than ever." I was miffed at his attitude. "I've already confirmed the date and time with Alex and with the community relations officer at Rampart. Between my morning appointments and my afternoon appointments I can run off a short announcement of the meeting on my computer and distribute it. And now everyone will want to come, if only to hear about the murder. If you're not doing anything, you could join us."

"I'm sure I can come up with a pressing engagement before Tuesday. Why are you so certain it was your jacket the corpse was wearing?"

"Because it had the initials FC on the sleeve. And I found out later it had the *Saints and Sinners* logo on the back. Couldn't be two of those."

"Do the police think this was your burglar?"

"I think it was. I don't know what they think. That's one reason for the Neighborhood Watch meeting, to find out what they think."

"Were you terrified—seeing a dead man in your jacket?"

"Not terrified." I stopped to think. "A little embarrassed. I had been talking about branding and mutilating the person who burglarized my house. And now he was dead in the street."

"You're not that powerful, dear."

"I know. But it was strange. And I'd never seen a bloody corpse before. Maybe I don't know what I feel."

"Maybe you're a little in shock. Other than that, Mrs. Lincoln, how did you enjoy the party?"

"I really did. Sort of." Nothing felt right. "Kirby McKenzie was there."

"Kirby McKenzie? As in your childhood sweetheart Kirby McKenzie? As in the star of *Shootout in Venice* Kirby McKenzie?"

"He wasn't my childhood sweetheart. We met in college."

"How is he?"

I wasn't sure what I wanted to say. "Fine, I think. Divorced. He said he'd call on Monday."

"I take back my comment about the murderer. Please, please, watch for the murderer. Just don't get reinvolved with Kirby McKenzie. Watching for the murderer has to be safer—for you—than seeing Kirby McKenzie."

"I don't think that's fair. I'm older, fatter, I hope wiser, and I'm certainly a different person. I think that seeing Kirby, at least once to tie up the loose ends, might be good for me."

"What would you say if a client—you—said that?"

"Michael, don't—" I stopped myself, because he was right. "I'd ask about drug use."

I chose truth over anger, but it wasn't an easy call.

"You're a good therapist, Faith."

"I don't know about that. Kirby was doing some coke, but it was a party. And all I had was one glass of wine."

"Okay."

"Okay what?"

"Okay, it's your life. When are you going to see him?"

"He said something about the beach on Wednesday. He's calling me Monday. A picnic at the beach isn't anything to worry about."

"Of course not. Nobody does drugs at the beach."

I didn't try to answer that.

"I have an appointment Tuesday afternoon to show some of Elizabeth's tapes to the ad agency that does the Elizabeth Taylor perfume commercials." Michael went right on as if he hadn't expected me to. "If I get free in time, I'll come to the Neighborhood Watch."

"What caused that decision?"

"That meeting will sport a stranger cast of characters than anything on television, with the possible exception of *3rd Rock From the Sun.* And being there will be more fun than hearing about it later."

"Thank you. See you Tuesday."

I had clients scheduled for ten, eleven, two, three, and four. When my eleven o'clock left, I microwaved a veggie burger to eat while I was running off the announcement, then headed for the street to leave it in mailboxes.

The day was clear and beautiful, and I was glad to have the opportunity to be out in it, even though I ended up getting a little more exercise than I had anticipated. Some of the mailboxes were on posts close to the street, but some were on pillars and trees close to the houses themselves, which meant climbing up and down stairs from the street, or cutting through yards that were mostly ivy or gazania.

At the beginning, I used the stairs. By the time I made my way all the way around to Alex and Wayne's duplex, I was stomping through ivy, hoping it was too early in the year for flea-infested rodents to be hiding in the undergrowth.

Even as I thought that, I was ashamed to be worried about fleas as I prepared to deal with crime. An amazing capacity for the trivial.

The only person who appeared to mark my trek was an Asian woman who peered around her drapes at me. I hoped she would be my first recruit. No one else seemed to notice me or care what I was doing.

Still, I was back in plenty of time for my two o'clock client. With a sense of accomplishment to boot.

I didn't hear from anyone over the weekend except Louie, and my sense of accomplishment had pretty much faded by the time Michael showed up on Tuesday evening. He was early, so we waited for Louie before cutting across Norman's gazania to the duplex.

Alex had set an automatic coffee maker and several trays of homemade cookies on the dining room table.

"If you want, you can have something stronger," he said.

Wayne greeted us from a corner by raising a glass in salute.

Michael, Louie, and I each declined anything but coffee.

"I'll be awake all night," I grumbled to Michael.

"All the better to watch the neighborhood," he replied.

The crime prevention specialist was the next to arrive. A nervous woman in her fifties with dyed red hair, face dusted powdery white, wearing a tailored suit and frilly blouse, she arranged some brochures on the coffee table. Alex had removed the copies of *Hunk* and cleaned the ashtray in preparation for the evening.

Officers Page and Davila, the same two officers who had knocked on Marcus's door four nights earlier, were the next to arrive. Christopher, who lived in the other half of the duplex, slipped in behind them.

"I hope it isn't going to be just us," I whispered.

"Be patient. Everyone will want to hear about the murder," Michael whispered. "Except Norman and Helena."

"They won't be in the same room with Louie or Marcus. And Louie and Marcus return the sentiment. It was Helena who called the police about the party."

"I told you this would be better than television— even if Christopher did decide to wear discreet earrings and a long-sleeved T-shirt instead of something that displays the Hawaiian floral arrangements on his arms."

"Is that what they are?"

"Who knows?" Michael shook his head. He was watching three elderly women slowly climbing the front steps. Two of them looked as if they had stepped out of a documentary on World War II refugees, with red-veined cheeks, kerchief-covered hair, and coats too heavy for the evening, under which were legs clad in thick cotton stockings.

They introduced themselves—Frieda and Martine— in thick German accents. Frieda, the older, a hawk-faced woman with a hearing aid and a cane, had leaned on her friend all the way up the stairs. Alex ushered them to the sofa and offered them coffee and cookies.

"We have lived in that house"—Frieda gestured with her cane—"for forty years, and no one has asked us over before. This was nice of you."

"I've lived up the block almost thirty years, and I could say the same," commented the third woman, Sybil. She had thin, overbleached hair and sad, pale eyes the same color as her washed-out khakis.

Page and Davila shook hands with each woman. Both officers were young, with the kind of bland faces that seemed overpowered by their uniforms.

The crime prevention specialist handed out the brochures.

Still another woman hurried up the steps, this one in her early thirties, with short brown hair, intelligent brown eyes, wearing shapeless gray sweats.

"Hi, I'm Carol," she said.

Alex offered her coffee, but she refused.

The last two neighbors, both men, arrived as Officer Page prepared to speak. Ramon, the younger of the two, introduced himself and Esteban.

"I didn't know the beaners were coming," Alex muttered.

"Careful, one of the officers is a 'beaner,' in case you didn't notice," I said, glaring at him. He glared back and blew smoke in my face. I sneezed.

"Gesundheit," Michael said.

Alex smiled.

I helped Ramon and Esteban to coffee and cookies, not quite trusting Alex to do it. Esteban was a small man with full, white hair and a matching mustache. Ramon looked as if he could be Esteban's son. He wore a white shirt with a dark tie, loosened at the collar, as if he had come straight from work.

Officer Page waited for everyone to settle down.

"I'm glad to see you all here tonight," he said. "We don't usually get this many people willing to organize a Watch."

"There was a murder in the street," Alex said. "We want to know about the murder."

"Yes sir, I can understand that." Page nodded at him, then shared the nod with the rest of the room. "There's not much I can tell you. We discovered a corpse in the street, about three houses down from here. The cause of death was a knife wound. We think the victim was actually stabbed near the southeast corner of the block, and he crawled this far in search of help before he died, maybe trying to get to the party, where people were. We haven't yet identified the body, but we're working on it."

"How can you not have identified the body?" I asked. "He was wearing my jacket."

"That doesn't necessarily make him the person who broke into your house. The prints on your window frame weren't clear enough to help us. They may not belong to the deceased. Anyway, the prints we got from the corpse weren't in our computer. We're still checking to see if they match prints in other computers or those from other crimes in the neighborhood."

Page said all that to me, then turned his attention again to the larger group.

"With luck, we'll at least be able to close the file on a few burglaries. We're not positive, but we think the murder may be gang-related. As you all know from the graffiti on this block, there's a lot of gang activity around here. Goes with the drugs."

"I thought gangs all had guns," Alex said.

Page ignored him and continued. "The gangs are the big drug dealers, and not just for this area. Those young, blond kids from the university drive up Hoover Street in their sports cars to buy marijuana, cocaine, heroine, whatever they want."

"Oh, my God," Frieda moaned. "Young people. Everything to live for. Why do they do it?"

Alex got up and headed for the kitchen.

I had given up my seat on the couch when the older women arrived. From my corner on the floor, I could see him take the bottle of Jack Daniels out of the cupboard.

"About the corpse," Michael said. "What about missing persons? Has anyone reported someone who matches the description missing?"

Page shrugged. "We think he might be Salvadoran, a member of a gang called Mara Salvatrucha, which just means big bunch of Salvadorans. The Salvadorans don't look at the police the way most citizens do. Where they come from, the police are agents of the government, and it's bad news when they show up. Salvadorans come here, but they don't try to fit in, and they won't call the police for anything. They particularly wouldn't call the police to report someone missing. If the guy was Salvadoran, it'll take forever for somebody to report him missing. We're talking to people in the community, though, and we hope to get something soon."

"What can we do?" Frieda asked.

"What you're doing now, ma'am," Page said. "Get to know one another. Keep your eyes open. If you see anything I ought to know about, call me."

"And just what will you do about it?" Alex asked.

"We'll get out here as soon as we can to check it out," Page told him calmly.

"And how soon is that?"

"That depends on what else is going on, what takes priority," Page replied. "We only have five cars to cover a lot of territory. With all the crime we have in Los Angeles, we have half the number of officers they have in Chicago, one third as many as New York."

"Then you ought to establish better priorities," Alex snapped. "What takes priority in my experience is hassling gays."

"Sounds like you've had a bad experience." Page was unruffled.

"Damn right. I was sideswiped, Saturday, making a left turn onto Alvarado, by some asshole in a blue Chevy who was running a red light. Pushed me over into oncoming traffic. I was goddamn lucky I didn't get hit again. Christopher was with me, and he almost had a heart attack." Alex waved his glass toward Christopher, who nodded solemnly. "Christopher has a history of heart trouble. He could have died."

"He's right," Christopher said, flashing the gold stud that pierced his tongue.

Page didn't blink.

"I chased the Chevy all over the neighborhood," Alex continued. "Then a cop pulled up behind me. I thought, great, help, but he wouldn't listen to what happened, didn't care about Christopher, called us a couple of fags, and gave me a ticket for speeding. Now, I may be gay, but I'm no fruitcake, and I wasn't the person who should have gotten the ticket. The guy in the Chevy should have gotten the ticket—for speeding, for reckless driving, for endangering the public—and the cop wouldn't go after him!"

A little of the Jack Daniels slopped over onto Alex's wrist. He stopped to lick it off.

"Well, sir," Page said, "I wasn't there, so I can't answer for the officer who was, but his name is on the ticket, and if you choose to go to court to protest the ticket, he'll have to appear. You have the right to do that, you know, you have the right to present your case to a judge."

"What the hell good is that going to do? Do you think any judge is going to find I'm right and a cop is wrong? In L.A.? Do you think I'm crazy?"

"No, sir, I just thought you wanted your rights."

"Goddamn right I want my rights!"

"Alex, we're getting off the subject," I said.

"Alex, there are ladies present," Wayne said, at almost the same moment.

Martine's jaw was agape, but Frieda didn't seem to have heard all of the outburst. Carol shook her head, amused. Sybil frowned.

"I'm sorry. Excuse me." Alex stormed back into the kitchen.

Page looked at the group.

"Are there any other problems that anyone would like to tell me about?"

"If not, let's get back to burglary and murder," I said.

"I don't have anything more to offer on that score," Page said. "But you have something to offer. Get to know who belongs on this block, who doesn't belong on this block, who's home during the day and who isn't. Get to know cars. About six hundred cars are stolen each month in the Rampart district, mostly Datsuns and Toyotas. Watch out for each other. If you see something you don't like, call me. I'm the senior lead officer for this area, and I want to know what's going on.''

"I always know when Faith is not home," Frieda volunteered. ''Those two brown cats sit out in front and wait for her.''

"Or you could have a billboard that says, 'The house is empty,''' Michael whispered.

Ramon had been translating for Esteban. Esteban whispered something back.

"There's a Toyota truck at the end of the block. Esteban says it's been there for several days. He saw some kids park it, mess around under the hood, and leave in another car," Ramon said.

"Thanks. We'll check it out. Anything else?" No one spoke. Page nodded, satisfied. "Okay. We'll turn the meeting over to the crime prevention specialist now.''

I walked the officers to the door, thanked them, and returned to my seat on the carpet. I had trouble listening to the woman gush about how much good we could do. The speech seemed designed for a different group.

When the woman ended by telling us to elect a block captain, I was surprised to discover that the group thought they already had one. I was it—the person responsible for setting up the next meeting and keeping them all in touch with one another.

In ones and twos, people picked up more pamphlets and window stickers and left.

Michael, Louie, and I were the last to go, except for Christopher. We said goodnight to Wayne, since Alex had never come back from the kitchen.

"That Alex, he's brave," Louie said, as we crossed back through the gazania.

"Did you think so?" I asked.

"Yeah. Talking back to the police like that. When he said, 'I may be gay, but I'm not a fruitcake,' that was all right." Louie chuckled.

"Goodnight, Louie."

Amy and Mac were waiting on the porch, just as Frieda said. They danced a little, expecting to go in, but Michael and I stood there until Louie had reached his back door.

"Alex and Wayne really are an unlikely couple," Michael said. "Alex is so in-your-face, and Wayne has that Confederate general quality."

"What do you mean?"

"Can't you see him—a Rock Hudson stand-in, wearing Johnny Reb grays? With that wavy hair and that smile? That touch of lost cause in his eyes?"

"I didn't know you found him that attractive," I said. "And unlikely as it may be, they are a couple."

"Such a shame. Louie may have thought Alex was brave. I, on the other hand, realized why another man might resort to gags." Michael kissed my cheek. "Good luck tomorrow. Call me if you need me."

"I don't need luck for a day at the beach."

"Then break a leg."

I watched him leave, then gathered up Amy and Mac and locked myself in for the night.

FOUR

KIRBY ARRIVED on my doorstep at quarter to two the following afternoon, bright and shiny and sober, massive torso ballooning over red bikini trunks. I was relieved to discover that the effect wasn't sexy, if that had been his intent. He was a little too pale, a little too hairy, and a little too heavy.

When I raised my hand in greeting, he caught it and kissed it. I was annoyed when the soft beard against my fingertips did, after all, remind me of sex.

"My God, you are beautiful," he rumbled. "How can you still have a body that looks like that? This is the most beautiful you have ever been in your life. While the rest of us are fading with time, becoming gray, bloated shadows of our youthful selves, you are gaining color and strength. You are the woman I always knew you would be. What a feckless fool I was to have left you."

"Kirby, I've gained weight, too," I said, smiling in spite of myself. "I'm too fat to wear a bikini anymore."

I stopped, because I didn't want to call attention to the fact that a bikini hadn't been his best choice. And the dark blue one-piece suit I was wearing tended to maximize what was still good about my body and hide the rest. The white lace jacket helped, too.

"And thank you for the compliment," I finished.

"Compliment? You are an incarnation of the Goddess, and we are going to the beach, where mortals will fall upon the sand at your feet in awe. And that will be tribute to your beauty."

I started to tell him he left me speechless, then discovered that he actually had. I couldn't find anything but a laugh. He was being romantic and silly at the same time, and he knew it.

He held out his arm.

Sweeping grandly down the stairs was the called-for gesture, but I had to check the house, get my straw beach bag, and set the deadbolt on the front door.

Kirby frowned at the bag. He leaned over to read the faded red letters on the side.

"Acapulco?" He straightened up, filled his chest with air. "I seem to remember Acapulco. I seem to remember that you tossed a bikini and a hair dryer into your purse and said, 'I'm going to Acapulco.'"

"I had a change of clothes and it was an overnight bag. And I had to go somewhere. You had just told me you were going on location, and that I could stay in the apartment as long as I wanted, as long as I had moved out by the time you got back." I hadn't expected him to remember. In fact, I hadn't thought of it when I threw towels and lotion into the old, colorful straw bag.

"And you obliged me. You were gone."

"Yes."

Kirby's eyes widened as he caught sight of something over my shoulder. I jerked around.

"A cat!" he exclaimed. "I know that cat! And my God, I'm seeing double!"

"You're not seeing double and you don't know that

cat," I said, still laughing, but now with relief. "You remember Tess, who died of old age at twenty, years ago. I got Amy when I first moved here, when a neighbor's cat had kittens. And because my parents had always insisted on neutering our cats, I decided to let Amy have a litter. It wasn't really a mature thing to do, but I did it anyway. I kept Mac, who looks just like his mother. And probably his father, too."

"I should get a cat," Kirby said.

"You should," I agreed. "Tess always liked you best."

Kirby held out his arm again, and this time I took it. We walked down the steps to a dark green Jaguar convertible with the license plate 4ASONG. I stopped to admire it, then got in when he opened the door for me.

"How long did you stay in Acapulco?" he asked as he pulled out into the street.

"A week. I was there for three days before I realized that all those men were paying attention to me because I was attractive, not because they felt sorry for me. And three days after that I was bored with the attention. I wanted to get back here and get on with my life, see what it was going to be like without you. Do you want a week-by-week description of the next fifteen years?"

"No. Just the highlight reel. Skip the wonderful time you were having with men paying attention to you."

"Truthfully, it took a while before I had a wonderful time with another man."

"But it happened."

"It did. I didn't take a vow of chastity, although I briefly considered taking the veil when I thought I'd never get over you."

Kirby downshifted the Jag to take the ramp onto the

Hollywood Freeway, then ran through the gears as he darted between cars into the fast lane and quickly back, to ease onto the Harbor Freeway.

"Same old panache," I said, holding onto my hair and wishing I had worn a hat. "I'll bet you just took thirty seconds off your record."

"Let me assure you, madame, that my old record stands. It was set one Friday morning at three a.m. after a two-day recording session, and it will not be broken soon. And sarcasm will not save you from answering the charge. You fell in love with someone else."

"You're right, Kirby, I did. I got over you. By the time I heard you had married Tara O'Brien, all I did was mist up a little. I was long past the full-scale histrionics."

"You're reminding me that I was the cause of misery in your life. Have you forgiven me?"

"I don't know. I'll have to think about it. I haven't thought about it in so long that I don't remember whether I've forgiven you or not."

He glanced over to catch my smile and cackled. "Could it be that in some small corner of your generous heart there is still a hint of feeling for me?"

"I don't think so, but I'll check and let you know later."

"You never married, did you? I would have heard, surely someone would have told me."

"No, I didn't."

"Why?"

A shadow passed in front of the sun, and I shivered. I waited until he had merged into Santa Monica Freeway traffic before I answered.

"Well, the easy answer is that the men I wanted to marry and the men who wanted to marry me were never the same. Beyond that, I guess I just couldn't see myself as someone's wife. Not even yours, although there were things I was willing to give when I lived with you that I haven't been willing to give since. I thought about getting engaged once, but it never happened." I bit my lip to keep from blurting out anything about that one.

"And you've lived alone all these years?"

"Yes." And been lonely sometimes, I added silently.

"You're stronger than I am. You always have been."

I didn't answer. I was pretty sure he was right.

The afternoon was the kind the Los Angeles Chamber of Commerce waits for, to send up the helicopters with the cameras for the promotional videos. The sky was a soft blue, with high, wispy clouds trailing like angel hair. As we sped west, the city became a blur of white cubes speared by palm trees, standing in a bright purple bowl.

Kirby hit a button on the cassette deck.

Buddy the Narc
waits in the park
by the slides,
he knows you'll be there.

I had to join in. *"You remember the guy, and the night he came by, to get high, now he lurks everywhere."*

"You know the words," Kirby said.

"Of course. I'm a fan. I must add, though, this particular song is something of a problem for me, with its pro-drug message.''

"It isn't pro-drug. It's anti-narc.''

"A fine distinction, don't you think?''

"Not at all. I wasn't advocating the use of drugs. I wasn't encouraging anyone to turn on, tune in, and drop out, or however that went. On the other hand, I've never denied using drugs recreationally. And I believe I have a constitutional right to use what are known as controlled substances in the privacy of my own home, or a friend's home, without having to worry that someone in attendance is only pretending to be my friend, and actually wants to do me damage. Narcs are scum—they betray trust.'' He downshifted again, passing a Mercedes and two BMWs.

"There's something to that, and I don't want to get stuck defending narcs. In the song, though, while you may not have said so in so many words, you made getting high sound like the thing to do. Drugs were the way to go.'' I scrunched down in the seat to avoid the wind, and I had to raise my voice to be heard.

"Well, that's true. Sex, drugs, and rock and roll,'' he shouted. "As I remember it, you used to get high occasionally.''

"I know. But that was a long time ago. And recently, my house was burglarized, probably for drug money, and then I found my coat on a dead man.''

"Ah. You're not really upset about drugs. You're upset about the things people do to pay for drugs.''

"Well, it's possible that you're right. But I could probably get upset about what drugs do to people, too.''

"To people who can't handle them.''

I resisted a surge of anger.

"Reality is for people who can't handle drugs," he chanted.

"I remember," I said. "I really do. But you're turning something important into something trivial."

"One of my many talents, madame."

"Yes it is, isn't it?" I hoped it wasn't one of mine.

We came to the end of the freeway and headed north along Pacific Coast Highway, with the cliffs of Santa Monica on the right and the beach and ocean on the left. Since it was a weekday, and the temperature was only in the seventies, there were only a few scattered bodies with bright swim trunks lying on towels on the gray sands. A few dogs, a few kites, a few sailboats. A quiet day.

I was sorry I had snapped at him.

He took a hard left into a parking lot. A young man with a deep tan came running over with one hand outstretched, the other pointing to a sign letting us know that parking wasn't free. Kirby pulled a bill out of his wallet and paid. The attendant trotted back the way he had come.

Kirby eased into a slot facing the ocean and turned off the engine. He looked at me.

"What do you need to say about the burglary?"

"That I feel bad. I feel violated, almost afraid to leave the house, as if every time I walk out the door I need to say goodbye to my life, because it may not be there when I get back. And when I come back, it's another reprieve, as I count cats and know everything is all right one more time. But it wasn't just the burglary. It was seeing that man dead and bloody in the street in my jacket. I feel as if the world is fragile." I reached for his hand. "Do you remember in the Buchner play, *Danton's Death,* the two gentlemen at the end of the first act? Walking around a puddle? And one of them says, you have to be careful, the earth's crust is thin here, you can fall through. That's the way I feel.''

He nodded. ''I understand.''

He shifted hands, so that he could put his arm around me, pulling my head to his shoulder.

''Your shoulder feels familiar,'' I said.

''It should.''

We held each other uncomfortably, across the divider between the bucket seats. He kissed me lightly, eyelids, cheek, mouth.

''Let's go,'' he said.

Kirby tossed his wallet into the trunk and retrieved a large towel and a small leather pouch. I pulled my wallet out of the straw bag and placed it near his. He slammed the trunk lid and reached for my hand.

''Let's find a place on the sand to dump our things and walk for a while,'' I said. ''This is such a lovely day.''

A Frisbee sailed high overhead, and we had to stop for a black Labrador in hot pursuit. The dog caught the disc in a spinning leap that Baryshnikov couldn't have matched, then trotted back to a couple of teenage boys, one of whom patted him on the head and sent the Frisbee sailing again.

''I like that dog,'' Kirby said, staring after him. ''I ought to get a dog like that.''

''Are you home enough to take care of a dog?''

''Probably not.''

We spread our towels several yards from the water, in tacit acknowledgment that the waves were high and white-capped, and neither of us knew which way the tide was moving. Kirby's towel was cardinal and gold, with the USC logo.

I laughed. "Who gave you that?"

"I gave some money to the school once, and the girl who took the pledge over the phone sent it to me in exchange for an autographed picture. I don't use it very often." He settled onto the towel. "Sit for a minute. Then we'll walk."

I sat crosslegged on my towel, a logo-less one with blue and green stripes, and turned my face up to the afternoon sun. I don't spend much time in the sun anymore. I'd forgotten how good it felt.

A breeze swiftly cooled the air.

Kirby took a joint out of the leather pouch, lit it, and held it out for me.

"I don't think so," I said.

He leaned over and blew smoke in my nose.

The aroma was sweeter than I remembered.

"How long has it been since you had a good time?" he asked.

"A while," I admitted.

I looked at him sideways, considering. I had nowhere to be and no reason to turn him down. I took his hand, allowing him to hold the joint for me.

"Yeah, okay." I popped the words through my vocal chords, holding the smoke in my lungs as long as I could.

"Okay, what?" He expelled a small amount of smoke.

"I'm not upset about drugs qua drugs. But there is something wrong somewhere, that people are so desperate for something that they steal from other people to get it."

"Not this stuff. People don't steal to buy a little grass."

"Probably not."

He took another hit and again held the joint for me.

"I'll tell you, though," I continued, still popping the sounds through my vocal chords, "this is not the same stuff that we used to smoke. This is a lot stronger, and it's not just because I'm older and I haven't smoked any in years that I think so. The stuff that we used to get, we used to have to smoke a whole joint to get high. Now, I've had two hits, and I'm beginning to lose my train of thought."

"More?"

I shook my head. "How do kids handle this?"

"Well, probably they don't very well." He sighed. "Do we have to get into it? You always had a cause. While everybody sane was sleeping in on Saturday with a hangover, you were walking the block distributing leaflets for some Assembly candidate."

"I remember that. He lost. He wanted to make a difference, and I thought he might. I had fantasies about running for office myself, making a difference in the way things happened. Didn't you ever want to make a difference in the world?"

"No. Let's walk."

Kirby stood and held out his hand. As I took it, he pulled me up and against him. I wanted to be miffed, but it seemed silly. I had a rush of feeling, of memory, of the two of us, how young we had been, and how much I had loved him.

"I think I'm going to get maudlin," I whispered.

"Oh, God, no, not that," he groaned. "Anything but maudlin."

"What're we going to do?"

"Walk. We'll walk it off."

"All right, but I have to leave my sandals here. I'll

keep my jacket, though.'' Making the decisions took a long time. ''Okay.''

We walked on a diagonal toward the water, swinging hands. The sand was warm between my toes, along the arches of my feet. Soft on top, giving a little when I stepped, then deadening. I wanted my feet to spring back, but they wouldn't.

Kirby kept tugging me toward the water. I kept tugging back, toward the rocks ahead of us. The water was too gray and icy looking. The afternoon sun rippled across the whitecaps, but I didn't want to go closer.

He started to cackle.

''Water. I want to go in the water.''

''Alone. You're going to go in alone.''

I struggled to release my hand from his grip. He squeezed it, then dropped it. He ran the few remaining steps into the waves, arms outstretched, and threw himself down.

I winced, certain he had landed belly first in the sand, but he somehow managed to start swimming. I followed him, slowly, until the first bit of cold water splashed my feet. The next wave hit my ankles. I stepped back, shivering.

When I looked back at the water, I couldn't see Kirby. Then I found white arms, farther out than I had expected. Too far, too far.

''Please come back,'' I whispered.

Finally, as I was starting to ache with fear for him, he turned.

He stood up near the shore and ran briskly to me.

''You look like the Great White Seal,'' I called, embarrassed that I had been so afraid.

"Arf! Arf!" He clapped his hands and shook himself.

"Wet!" I shrieked. "I'm getting wet! Cold and wet! Aaaagghhh!"

He grabbed me and kissed me, wet beard against my mouth, wet body cold all the way down mine.

"You're still my baby darling," he murmured.

"No, I'm not. And for a minute I felt like Mrs. Norman Main."

He stiffened, dropped away from me.

"Thank you, Judy Garland," he announced.

"I'm sorry. I shouldn't have said that."

"No."

"Well, pfffffft." I tried to regain the moment before. "You shouldn't have swum out so far."

"You're right." He smiled and took my hand again.

We started toward the rocks, wet hands entwined. The day had become grayer, the sky turning the color of the water.

The rocks were black and pock-marked. From a distance, I had thought it might be fun to climb them. Up close, I felt I would just be adding dirty to cold and wet. And the gray waves with the white foam were getting higher.

"Do you think we left our things too close to the water?" I asked.

"What? I don't know," he answered, raising his eyebrows in mock astonishment, eyes darting about. "Why—why—our things could be getting moist—perhaps damp—even as we speak. Certainly, we should return to the towels and check."

"Gee, what a good suggestion."

We walked back to the towels, clasped hands swinging. But Kirby stopped short.

"Food," he muttered. "Food and drink. Why didn't I bring nectar? Or at least beer? Oh, what a rogue and peasant slave am I!"

"Well, that may be true, but we could go somewhere else and do something about food and drink anyway. Besides, it's getting too cold and windy to stay."

I shook out my towel and picked up my sandals and bag. We trudged back to the parking lot.

"What would you like?" he asked.

"Does that mean Chinese or Italian?"

"No, woman, no. It does not. It means the world."

"I'm too hungry to wait for it to cook. What would you say to Henri's?"

"I'd say you have great taste in seafood and a long memory."

"And you'd be right," I replied.

The drive back from the beach was slow, as the Jaguar was caught in afternoon traffic. Kirby barged from one lane to another, but none of them moved. We were both coming down from the effects of the joint and beginning to get grumpy by the time he dropped me off to shower and change.

I swallowed a cup of yogurt in three bites to ease the hunger pangs, then put down food for the cats, enough to tide them over if I came in late. Not too late. I couldn't stay out too late. On Thursday morning I had to be at the clinic, sharp and rested and in time for a ten a.m. appointment.

Showering and dressing took almost the full hour, even though the effects of the marijuana had pretty much worn off. But Kirby didn't live far.

His house was on one of the winding streets north of Los Feliz Boulevard, in the hills west of Griffith Park. As I parked the Taurus in front of the wrought iron gate, I wondered what had prompted him to buy this particular building. It seemed overdone, too heavy, too much stucco, too much tile, an imitation Spanish mansion that imitated all the wrong things.

I walked down the steps from the street into a concrete courtyard with a dry concrete fountain. Between the hillside and the trees, the house would have to be dark most of the time, despite the high windows.

The front door was open.

"Hello," I called.

"Be right there," he answered.

I walked into what would have been a living room if someone else had owned the house. Kirby had turned it into a music room with a grand piano, a set of drums, and one token sofa. The hardwood floor gleamed, polished for dancing. Over the fireplace, a stuffed boar's head leered at me, a jaunty gold hoop dangling from one ear.

"Let's go," Kirby said, suddenly appearing in an archway.

He held out a lit joint, and I took a hit without thinking.

We kissed lightly, and I followed him out and back up the stairs to the garage. He flicked the remote, and the door rose. I waited until he had backed the Jaguar into the street before getting in.

Henri's was at the foot of the hill, and had been since 1949, according to the sign. The chef had bought it when the original owner retired. The seafood was always fresh, the salads tossed at the table, the wine cellar impressive, and guests were encouraged to linger after dinner over concoctions of brandy-laced coffee into which a flaming orange peel was dropped, the fire then smothered with whipped cream.

I had been there often with Kirby, then sporadically with other people after we broke up. The restaurant had never changed, stubbornly resistant to the tides of the L.A. food trends. I had always felt comfortable there.

Once upon a time, the maitre d' would have recognized me. But this one was young, and he bowed only to Kirby. He showed us to a table in the back room.

"Everyone looks so old," I whispered to Kirby after the waiter had taken our order.

"They've probably all been coming here for twenty years," he whispered back. "I think I remember the couple in the corner from our first date."

The spinach salad was warm and tangy and crunchy, the salmon fresh, the sorrel sauce light, the baby vegetables perfectly fanned on the plate. I had forgotten what a sensual pleasure it was to eat when stoned. The champagne bubbled in my nose. And the coffee with brandy was deeper and richer and more complex than I remembered.

Kirby drove carefully back up the hill. I leaned against him, nuzzling his earlobe. I disengaged long enough for him to park, but I was considering what it would be like to be reacquainted with the contours of his body as we walked down into the courtyard.

A small mass was huddled against the front door.

"Hey, dude, I thought you'd never get here," the lump said.

"Tigger, what's happening?"

"Oh, nothing. I just thought you might like to play for a while."

"Yeah, sure. You're alone?"

"Yeah."

"Where's Janie?"

Tigger shrugged. "Who knows, dude? Who knows?"

Kirby cackled. "Tigger, this is Fay."

I didn't bother to correct him. I didn't plan on knowing Tigger long enough for it to make any difference what he called me.

Kirby unlocked the door. Tigger and I followed him into the music room.

"You don't mind, do you, Fay? If we play a little while?"

"Hey, no. I'd like to hear you." The combination of the alcohol and the coffee and the dope had made my head a little fuzzy. But I did want to hear him play.

"Great. Get yourself a drink, Tigger. I'll give Gordo and Ray a call, see if they'd like to come over."

They must not have lived far, because Kirby had no sooner handed me a glass of wine than Gordo was grabbing me and swinging me around, which didn't help my fuzzy head. I giggled.

"Jesus, Fay," Gordo said. "It's good to see you. If you and Kirby had had a kid when you first started sleeping together, he'd be a teenager now."

"And I would have raised him alone," I answered, sober for a moment.

Gordo just laughed. And moistened the mouthpiece of his trombone.

Ray brought an acoustic guitar and a friend, a thin girl with long dark hair who promptly passed out on the couch.

Tigger had taken over the drums, marking little rhythms while he waited.

"Let's have a little toot before we start," Kirby said. He had a small glass vial of white powder in one hand, a tiny spoon in the other.

When he came to me, I held first one nostril, then the other, and inhaled deeply. The world snapped into sparkling clarity.

The boar's head winked at me.

Kirby sat down at the piano and motioned me over. I settled beside him on the bench, fascinated by the black keys, and the white keys, by his fleshy hands that looked so heavy and were suddenly so light.

I took a sip of the wine. It tasted so good, so light, so smooth. And it would be my last glass of the evening. I would switch to water.

"We'd be lying if we said we don't talk about the girls, talk about the ladies, talk about the babies," he sang.

I hadn't heard that song before. It struck me as odd, I had to really listen to it, because I would never have guessed that Kirby said anything more intimate to his male friends than, "Hey, man, let's play."

"And I dream about my mother, though she's gone," he wailed in his rich, throbbing baritone.

I would have to ask him about that. His mother was still alive. I wanted everyone to leave so that I could hold him and ask him about that. I didn't want him to sing for anyone else. I took another sip of wine.

And one song segued directly into another. Tigger and Gordo and Ray evidently knew all of Kirby's music. They stopped only to share the cocaine, and to refill the glasses all around.

The last thing I remembered was the boar's head, with its glittering, winking eyes.

FIVE

TIGGER WAS DRUMMING inside my head. Snare drum, bass. Snare drum, bass. The same riff over and over. The bass was in my left eye, and I wanted to scream whenever he hit it. But I couldn't make a sound. My mouth was so dry it was stuck shut.

Concentrating between the riffs, I moved the sound outside my head, but the pain stayed inside. I began to feel other things, all unfamiliar. The mattress was too soft, the sheets too smooth. And someone was next to me. That was the noise. Someone was snoring.

Please stop, I whimpered, but the words were only in my head.

The thought that if I opened my eyes, I would know where I was burbled up through the ooze of my brain cells. I tried the right eye first. Dark. Wherever I was, it was dark. Not quite dark. A slit of light came through between the panels of heavy drapes that covered the wall to the side of the bed. I shut my right eye again, then tried both of them.

At first they wanted to go in different directions, but I convinced them to work together. Even so, they didn't focus on anything but the sheet and the down comforter. I would have to roll over onto my back. Maybe even sit up.

Rolling over on my back set the cymbals crashing.

No. I didn't do this anymore. I didn't do shit and wake up with a hangover. Not ever.

Not ever, the cymbals echoed.

But I had.

I had to determine who was in bed with me. All I could see was hair. Focusing both eyes carefully through the pain, I could tell that some of it was beard.

Kirby. I was in bed with Kirby. Presumably his bed, in his bedroom.

I shut my eyes again, but the bass drum in my left eye wasn't going to stop pounding as long as he snored.

What had happened? How did I get to bed? Where were my clothes?

Blank. All blank.

I opened my eyes again, and this time spotted the teal blouse and pants I had been wearing the night before, tossed over a chair in the corner of the room. Had we made love, for the first time in fifteen years, while I was a zombie? I tried to remember. I would have to ask him, some other time.

I eased myself upright. Tigger did a solo in my head totally unrelated to Kirby's snoring.

One foot on the floor, then the other, as someone with size thirty-six boots went clunk, clunk in my brain.

When the vibrations stopped, I stood up. One step at a time, toward the window.

I thought I screamed when I peeked through the curtains, but no sound came out. I had forgotten to unstick my mouth.

Bright daylight. It was bright daylight out there. I shut my eyes and clutched the drapes.

One step at a time, toward the chair. I put on my

underwear. No purse, no shoes. I picked up the blouse and pants and moved toward the bedroom door. My head throbbed in its own rhythm, sometimes in step with my feet, sometimes on to a different drummer.

The door opened into a short hallway. Stairs—Mexican tile stairs—led down to my left. Light blazed in cruelly through an open door to my right. A closed door was straight ahead.

Eureka. Beyond the closed door was a bathroom.

I ignored the middle-aged hag in the mirror, the one with dry skin and puffy eyes and flaking makeup, as I rinsed my mouth and splashed my face before putting my blouse and pants on. The water made me gag. My stomach knotted, then settled.

I blew my nose on some toilet paper, hoping to clear my sinuses and get rid of any residue of cocaine, but it didn't help.

The living room—music room—was at the bottom of the stairs. My shoes were under the piano bench, and my purse was leaning against one leg.

Ray and the girl with the long dark hair were asleep on the couch, fully clothed.

I fumbled with the lock on the front door and stumbled into the courtyard. The sun didn't hit me until I started up the stairs to the street.

I searched my purse frantically for dark glasses, whimpering as I realized I had left them at home, afraid I would shrivel like Dracula in the glare.

But I made it to the car. The clock in the Taurus said 9:35, and I had to think about what that meant. Not enough sleep, for one thing. God only knew what time I had passed out. It would take a day or two to unjangle my circadian rhythms after this.

The engine roared in my ears, setting off the drums

and cymbals again. Fortunately, home was close. Down the hill, two miles, up the next one.

The garage door opening sounded like an earthquake—the Big One.

Then up the stairs, one at a time.

Someone was waiting. A Latina, maybe forty, sitting on the top step, stood up. Drew herself erect. She was just over five feet tall and about three feet wide. Her pink and white striped blouse vibrated like a tweed suit on television.

"Faith, right?" Her voice boomed and echoed.

"Right."

"Good. I was afraid I missed you, that you'd left early for the clinic. Esteban said on Thursday you go to the clinic."

Shit.

"It is, and I'm in a hurry," I said.

"But they arrested Jorge."

"What?"

"My son, Jorge."

"I'm sorry. I don't know what you're talking about."

"I'm Graciela, Graciela Carrasco."

The woman held out her hand. I took it limply, trying to figure out how to get past her, get inside, out of the sun, get to the phone to call the clinic. And get water. My mouth was too dry to talk.

"Esteban, my husband, said I should talk to you."

"You live across the street?"

Graciela nodded. "Esteban came to that meeting, he met you, and he said I should talk to you. They arrested our son, Jorge. They say he killed the man in the street the other night. This is not true. My son is not a member of a gang, the way they say he is. You will help us, okay?"

"I don't know what I can do." Tigger was doing his Ginger Baker imitation against the back of my left eye. I had to shut it. "Why are you coming to me?"

"Esteban said you are the captain of the block. You're in charge. You'll take care of this."

I silently cursed Ramon's translation. "Okay, I'm the block captain, but that doesn't mean—"

I had to stop to figure out what it did mean. It meant that I was trying to foster some sense of community in a group of people with nothing in common except that they happened to live on the same block. Graciela stood there, waiting for me to continue, and blocking my way to the phone. And water. And shade.

"Okay," I said. "I'll call Officer Page and see what I can find out for you."

Amy brushed against my ankles, waiting. Mac stared at me from the corner of the porch, sad eyes telling me that all the food from the day before was gone.

"Okay." Graciela nodded. "You talk to him, you tell him this is a mistake, Jorge is a good boy, he didn't do this. I got to go to work now. I'm late, but they will understand when I tell them you will help my son."

Graciela trudged off, shopping bag on her arm.

I was inside the house gulping water, hoping my churning stomach would let it stay down, before the woman was halfway down the steps.

I used my office phone to call the clinic.

"I have a splitting headache, and I'm not going to be able to make it in until this afternoon," I told Mary, the clinic receptionist. That was close enough to the truth. "Can you get hold of my ten o'clock and my eleven o'clock? If either one needs to see me, I can reschedule for tomorrow, this week only.''

"Betty Fulton is homeless, you know that, Faith. No way I can get hold of her. And Elena Ortiz has probably left her house. But I'll do the best I can. You sound awful.''

"I feel awful. Tell them I'm sorry. I owe them. See you at two.''

I was angry even as I hung up quietly, angry with myself for disappointing my clients, angry with them for leaning on me. And it wasn't as if I got anything out of this. I was volunteering my time.

I scrubbed the remainders of makeup from my face, or at least what hadn't already soaked into my pores, to remain there until flushed out at my next facial. I swallowed two aspirin tablets with another glass of water, fed the cats, and lay down on the bed. Amy hopped up and stretched out beside me, and Mac tried to work his way between us.

The phone rang, jolting every sinew in my body. Mac leapt off the bed in terror, and Amy retreated to the foot. I found the receiver without opening my eyes.

"Could you make it in by noon?'' Mary asked. "Elena is here. She says she doesn't mind waiting, and she really wants to talk to you. You might want to know that there are fresh bruises on her face. Some john got rough with her.''

"Okay. Tell her I'll be there.''

"Then maybe I could reschedule Betty Fulton for one.''

I wanted to say no, that I couldn't see all those people without a break, but guilt overcame me, and I agreed.

The dial tone buzzed in my ear. I was grateful for

that, the only sound in my ear. The aspirin had begun to work, and the drums in my head were starting to slow down. I replaced the receiver and considered opening my eyes.

I did so just long enough to set the radio alarm for one hour. Then I shut them again.

The hour wasn't long enough, but at least when the music came on—soft jazz, thank God—the pain in my head no longer made me want to whimper.

I tried my eyes, one more time.

Midmorning sun slipped gently through the priscillas, which were freshly laundered and free of the blood spatters left by the burglar. The shadow of a trellis with a climbing rose partly covered one window, the one with shiny new glass. The rose should be blooming better. I hadn't pruned it enough in the fall.

The view from the other window was a wire fence almost entirely engulfed by a very healthy white wisteria. The vines cast shadowy patterns on the dusty rose and ivory bedcover. I was glad the shadows weren't bars. I didn't want to have bars on the windows.

My bedroom. For years now my cocoon. But this day I couldn't sleep long enough for metamorphosis. I would have to go forth as a caterpillar.

Two pink and yellow Peace roses stood in a glass bud vase on the night stand, along with a brass lamp, a clock radio, and a phone. I couldn't smell the flowers, although I knew they were fragrant. My sinuses were still clogged from the night before.

"I don't do that anymore," I said aloud. "And I won't see Kirby again."

I rolled out of bed and made it to the shower.

The water helped.

I would rather have gone back to bed than gotten

dressed for the clinic, but I forced myself to keep going. Coffee was next, Cuban coffee from the mini-espresso maker. And that helped, too.

Makeup was difficult, because my eyes were so puffy. Probably better that I look a little ill, though. And better not to dress too much. Jeans and a sweat shirt would do.

At quarter to twelve, I was ready to leave for the clinic. Sometimes I walked the four blocks. This time I drove.

The small medical clinic took up the equivalent of two stores in a minimall on Sunset. Other inhabitants included a Cuban bakery, a discount outlet for packaged goods, a grocery store with produce that was cheaper and riper than could be found in the supermarkets—although sometimes beyond ripe to rotten—and a store that promised inexpensive fashions for women and children.

I made quick stops at the bakery and the grocery, picking up a guava jelly and cheese-filled pastry and more coffee at the first and a couple of tangerines at the second. I was the only Anglo in both stores.

"Are you okay?" Mary asked when I pushed through the door to the clinic, purse over my shoulder, paper bags in my hands. Mary's eyelids, heavy with mascara, crinkled in worry.

Mary was an unlikely receptionist, a twentysomething with fuchsia hair and a nose ring, wearing a white jacket over her tank top and flowered skirt. She was reliable, though, and bilingual.

"No," I answered. "But I think I can make it through the afternoon."

I would be of more use to the clinic if I spoke Spanish, I knew that, and sometimes I thought about taking lessons. I also knew that not taking lessons was a way of avoiding volunteering more time.

Elena Ortiz was sitting on a sofa. She was young and attractive, or would have been without the bruises.

"I am so sorry, Faith," she said. "You are not feeling well. I shouldn't have asked you to come in."

"It's all right." I felt guilty that Elena had heard me. "As long as you don't mind if I eat and drink in front of you."

"It's okay."

I led Elena into the small office that was mine on Tuesdays and Thursdays. The cramped clinic had been partitioned into cubicles that were barely more than closets. This particular one contained two easy chairs and a table with a box of tissues. Anything else I needed I was expected to bring with me when I came and take away when I left.

I settled down to listen to Elena, ignoring my aching sinuses and throbbing eyes.

After Elena Ortiz there was Betty Fulton, and then four more clients. I took one break to get a bowl of corn and tomato soup at the restaurant where Michael and I had eaten lunch the week before, which caused me to be late for my three o'clock. But the day finally came to an end.

"I know it was a tough afternoon for you," Mary said as I left. "But thanks for coming in. And take care of yourself."

I nodded and promised, her compassion increasing my guilt over my dereliction of duty.

I drove the four blocks home feeling sorry for myself. And only when the car was in the garage and I was climbing the stairs to the house did I remember my promise to call Officer Page.

There were two messages on my answering machine from clients who wanted to talk with me and one from Kirby. I called Officer Page first and was surprised when I actually reached him.

"Late afternoon is the best time to get me," he explained. "I get busier in the evening. What can I do for you?"

"Graciela Carrasco asked me to call," I told him. "She said you arrested her son, Jorge, for the murder. She wanted me to tell you she doesn't believe he did it."

"Yeah, sure she doesn't," Page said. "We got a tip, though. A witness came forward, said he saw him with the body, recognized him. And the Carrasco boy admits to being there, he just denies the crime. But we found a bloody shirt in his room. Did his mother tell you that?"

"No. Did the blood match the victim's?"

"Match on type. Getting the DNA will take a while."

"What about the weapon?"

"The knife was still in the body. No clean prints."

"Can you tie the knife to Jorge?" I wanted to end the questions, but I had to ask. I was tired. I had been asking questions and listening to answers for hours, and I wanted to take a nap. At the same time, I didn't want to face Graciela Carrasco without all the answers I could get.

"No, but there's nothing unusual about the knife. No reason it couldn't be his."

"What about a motive?"

"Gang-related is still our best bet."

"Only if Jorge was a member of a gang. His mother says he wasn't."

"All those Mexican kids are gang members. Mothers don't always know."

"Cuban. The Carrascos are Cuban. They're political refugees, not economic ones. They're middle class. That makes a big difference in whether kids join gangs. And that goes for the Mexican kids, too." I stopped. Page either knew all that or he didn't. I wondered if he made racist noises around Davila, his partner.

"The kid has a court-appointed attorney, ma'am." Page was still unflappable. "If you have any information that might help him, maybe you should talk to her."

"Can you give me her name and phone number?" A brief conversation with the attorney would prove to Graciela Carrasco that I had done everything possible.

Page left the line for a moment.

"Her name is Miriam Stern." He gave me the number.

I thanked him and said goodbye. I tried the number, but Miriam Stern had left for the day. The young, female voice who had answered as "Law Offices" took a message.

The two client messages still had to be returned. One was from the night before. I was relieved when I got answering machines on both. And Kirby could wait.

I went back to the bedroom, lay down, and shut my eyes.

One more time, the phone jolted me upright and scattered the cats.

"I want to know all the exciting details about seeing Kirby McKenzie again," Michael said.

"Actually, you probably don't."

"Why wouldn't I?"

"Because it turned into a very long night, and I don't remember all of it."

Michael was silent.

"Don't judge me, goddamn it," I snapped.

"You mean you haven't already judged yourself?"

"That's different. Anyway, it was a one-time thing. I slipped. Anyone could slip when confronted with that kind of situation, seeing someone she had been involved with when she was young. Especially after the burglary and the body in the street." I had been rehearsing that line all afternoon, in between clients.

"Especially when she doesn't have much of a life except her work and hasn't had for more than three years, ever since she was psyched out by the psych professor," Michael said. "If you're not feeling young today, you've probably punished yourself more seriously than anyone else would have."

"Thank you, I guess. Does that mean I'm absolved?"

"If you want me to say, 'Go forth and sin no more,' I'll say it. 'Go forth and sin no more.' Did that do it?"

"I don't know. I hope. Kirby left a message on my machine, and I have to call him and tell him I'm not going to see him again."

"Good for you. Did you make it through your day at the clinic?"

"More or less. You might also be interested in knowing that the police arrested a kid who lives across the street for the murder. You remember Esteban, the guy with the white mustache?"

Michael made a noise of assent.

"His son," I continued. "His mother asked me to tell the police he isn't guilty."

"What a wonderful idea. His mother will think

you're terrific. And with the killer locked up, you can safely continue with your Neighborhood Watch group. I like it."

"But Jorge may not have done it. There is a presumption of innocence in these things."

"Oh, come on, Faith. Most of the people the police arrest are guilty, you know that. I appreciate the right to presumption of innocence as much as anyone. But you have to admit that it's clogging our courts."

"I've left a message for his attorney. And I'm sure she'll recommend a plea bargain if she thinks he's guilty. To keep the case from clogging the courts." I was annoyed, and my head was starting to ache again. "Have you heard from the Elizabeth Taylor perfume people?"

"No, and I don't expect to for a week or two. These things take time. I caught the subject change, and I won't toss it back. Do you want to have brunch on Sunday?"

"That sounds fine."

We arranged time and place.

I had barely replaced the received when the phone rang again. I considered ignoring it, but it was most likely one of the two clients, and I didn't want to play telephone tag with them.

"You left." Kirby's voice was still hoarse with hangover. "I thought, when I fell into bed beside you, barely brushing your naked shoulder with my lips, not wanting to disturb you, that I would experience the joy, the ecstasy, of waking up and finding my angel here with me once again. But I woke instead to desolation. The loneliness of cold sheets in an empty bed. Not even a note. Although, for the record, a note would not have compensated for the loss of a fantasy. And then you ignored my message.''

"I'm sorry. I just got back from the clinic, and I haven't had a chance to call you. I didn't think about leaving a note. Kirby, what happened last night? How did I end up naked in your bed?''

"At some absurd hour of the morning, you suddenly slumped against me. Since sending you home was out of the question, Gordo and I carried you up the stairs and placed you gently on my bed, fully clothed. I returned sometime later to find you between the sheets, your clothes tossed carelessly over a chair. Since no one had entered the bedroom, I can only assume that you awoke long enough to make yourself comfortable.''

"Ah. Okay. I woke up this morning with the mother of all hangovers, one that eclipsed all the memories of the good old days, and I couldn't remember anything beyond the piano bench.''

"I thought it might be that bad. To confess my baser impulses, I did try to wake you when I got into bed.''

"Do you do that a lot?''

"Try to wake you? No, madame, clearly I do not, since the last time must have been close to fifteen years ago.''

"I mean stay up all night playing and drinking and doing a lot of dope.''

I waited through the silence.

"I entertain frequently,'' Kirby said finally, "and I am known as a good host. My substance use has changed very little over the years. You seem to have lost your tolerance.''

I thought about which way to take that.

"I want to see you, Fay," he continued. "Soon. Have you eaten? We could have dinner tonight."

"I'm feeling pretty lousy, Kirby." I tried to formulate the sentence, the one that would tell him I couldn't see him again.

"Then Saturday. Oh, yes, baby darling, Saturday. Saturday is my father's birthday, and you know how he has always loved you. Come with me for dinner Saturday night, just Evan and Dixie and Chas and Phyllis and you and me."

"I'd love to see Evan and Dixie, I really would. I've always loved them, you know that." I tried to come up with something to say about Chas, Kirby's brother, and his wife Phyllis, but Kirby saved me.

"Then it's done. We're meeting at Les Etoiles at eight. I'll add one to the reservation. Come over here at six, we'll have a drink and drive over together."

I struggled with a refusal. But I truly wanted to see Evan and Dixie. And talking to Kirby in person would be easier than telling him over the phone.

"Okay," I said. "I'd like that. I'll see you Saturday."

Long after I hung up the phone, I was still sitting on the bed thinking of Evan and Dixie. Evan McKenzie and Dixie Shayne. I had thought of them every time I saw either of their names in the Calendar section of the *Times*, doing occasional television guest spots, or making rare stage appearances. One of the great acting partnerships of all time. And my judgment on that hadn't been colored by my love for them.

My earliest memory of the pair—years before I met Kirby—was from their long-running television series, *The Thin Man*. And the *film noir* version of *MacBeth* they had made was a cult favorite, still showing up from time to time in art houses.

I had met Kirby in my junior year in college, when we were cast in a production of *Two for the Seesaw* that a mutual friend was directing as a master's project. I moved in with him two weeks after the show closed.

My fantasy of happily-ever-after with Kirby had been one of living together and working together, just like Evan and Dixie. The four of us would be a small, happy family.

But Kirby didn't want that role. He wanted to quit school and work professionally, on his own. Dixie and I had pressured him to finish his last year. He had done so, and I wasn't sure if he had forgiven either of us. Three years later, when he was leaving to go on location in a highly forgettable Western, made in one of those slumps when Westerns weren't pulling audiences, he decided he wanted to live alone.

I had called Dixie after I found my own apartment, hoping to see her, hoping we could stay friends. Dixie had told me gently that my only place in the McKenzie family had been as Kirby's friend. If Kirby and I reconciled, Dixie would be delighted to see me. In the meantime, it simply wasn't possible.

I almost called Kirby to tell him I had changed my mind about dinner Saturday. But really, we needed to talk. And surely he would stay straight around Evan and Dixie.

I would see him one more time and then get on with my life.

SIX

MIRIAM STERN CALLED just after nine in the morning, waking me up. Twelve hours of sleep had barely repaired the worst of the self-inflicted damage from Wednesday night.

"I believe Jorge," Miriam Stern said, after I told her who I was and how the visit from Graciela Carrasco had prompted the call. "I don't think he did it. And I can use any help I can get. I have a few minutes at one o'clock. You want to stop by?"

I hesitated. That would be cutting it close for my two o'clock appointment with Jack Griffin. But otherwise I would have to put off meeting the attorney until Monday. Doing it today, I could report back to Graciela with a clear conscience and forget about it.

"I'll be there," I said.

In fact, because I was anxious to get the meeting over with, I arrived at the law offices ten minutes before the scheduled time. Miriam Stern, however, was late.

The waiting room was tiny, dimly lit, with an opaque green rippled window shielding the receptionist from visitors. I sat on a worn plaid couch, too restless to pick up a tattered *Time* magazine. Some older places in downtown L.A. are chic, some funky, some cry out to be restored. This office and the building housing it were simply old and ugly.

When Miriam Stern opened the door and held out her hand, I thought for a moment that she was a secretary. She seemed too young and too short to be an adult. The thin forearms that stuck out from the sleeves of her tailored blouse were covered with fine, dark hair. Her black eyes were clear, startling even without makeup. A strong jaw thrust out from a face dusted with freckles, framed by about two inches of bristly black curls.

I took the offered hand and introduced myself.

She led me past the cramped area that held the receptionist's desk and some file cabinets and into what seemed to be a combination conference room and library. We sat down on two padded leather chairs in a nook between bookshelves. She didn't bother to offer me coffee.

"Okay, here's the situation," she said, leaning toward me. She had a trace of a New York accent, just enough to sound a little tough. "Jorge says he was coming home from a party—I've verified the party—and he saw a body lying in the street, all curled up. He says he touched the body, turned it over, wanting to help, and then realized whoever-it-was was already dead. He got blood on his hands and, without thinking, wiped the blood on his shirt. He was afraid to call the cops. He stuffed the shirt in a corner of his closet, where the cops found it."

"That sounds believable to me."

"Yeah, to me, too. But the ADA says they have a witness, somebody who is willing to come into court and say he or she saw Jorge do it. The ADA has to disclose the identity to me before the trial, but right now he's being coy, hoping we'll give in and bargain. Besides, he's arguing that if the witness is identified, there might be a problem with gang members retaliating.''

''That would only be true if Jorge were a member of a gang. His mother says he isn't.''

''No, but there is evidence that a couple of gangs have been moving into your area, Mara Salvatrucha and the Temple Street Gang. The ADA is offering a theory that Jorge was being pressured to join, that the murder was some kind of initiation, which was why it was done with a knife rather than a gun.''

''What did Jorge say?''

''That the ADA is wrong.''

''Then why does he think Jorge is lying?''

Miriam Stern studied my face.

''You seem ready to jump to his defense,'' she said. ''How well do you know him?''

''I don't. I suppose I've seen him coming and going over the years, but I'm not sure I'd recognize him. It's just that his parents seem like nice people, honest people, and I'm trying to organize a Neighborhood Watch, and I thought that talking to the police, and talking to you, might help foster a sense of community.'' That sounded lame, but I didn't have a better answer, at least not without going into a long story about the burglaries.

''People don't do this in L.A., you know that.''

''Do what?''

''Help out neighbors, especially not across ethnic lines.''

''Well, I'm not really doing very much.''

''You want to do more?''

''I'm not sure. What did you have in mind?''

''Obviously, someone trusts you, or Mrs. Carrasco

wouldn't have asked you to serve as go-between with the police.''

I shrugged. "It's either trust or a poor translation of Neighborhood Watch block captain.''

"Whatever." Miriam smiled, a flash that only briefly replaced her regular half-scowl. "In any case, she came to you. So maybe somebody else on the block would trust you enough to talk, if you went to them. And we could find out what this witness actually saw.''

"You want me to ask questions.''

"Right.''

"Why don't you send a detective?''

"I don't have a lot of money to spend on detectives. And I don't have time to go myself. And you're already there. A familiar face. A trusted face. And you're a psychologist—you're trained to ask questions. You're my best shot.''

"I don't know." I tried to come up with a way to refuse. "Do you even know whether the witness lives on the block?''

"No—but the witness evidently knew where Jorge lived.''

"That doesn't really narrow it down. What time was he spotted?''

"The police discovered the body at 11:37 p.m., according to the report, and time of death wasn't much earlier. Maybe an hour, tops. So you're looking for somebody who was on the street, or looking out the window at the street, between ten thirty and eleven thirty." Miriam stopped and waited.

"Will Jorge get out on bail?''

"No. The judge refused bail. The ADA somehow convinced him that Jorge was a flight risk, even though he was born in L.A. and his whole family lives here.''

She smiled again, the same brief flash. "So you'll help?"

"I'll ask a few questions. On the block. Just the people who came to the Neighborhood Watch meeting. And I'll ask about the people at the party, the one I had gone to, the one the police broke up. Some of them may have been regular visitors." I thought about Denise.

"Great. That's a start." Miriam Stern stood up and held out her bony hand again. "And I think you should meet Jorge. I'll leave word at the jail that you're his therapist."

I started to argue, but it didn't seem worth it.

"Thanks for coming," she said. "Can you find your way out?"

I found my way out. I rushed home as quickly as downtown traffic allowed, only to find Jack Griffin waiting on the porch.

"You're late!" he yelled as I started up the steps. "I've been here a good fifteen minutes! And this is your home! Why the hell can't you be on time when I'm coming to your home?"

I was quiet until I was level with him, figuring out the best way to handle the situation.

"I'm sorry," I said, wishing I were three inches taller and a body builder. "I didn't intend to be late. I had another obligation, and I thought I could take care of it and be back here on time."

"I don't give a shit about your other obligation! I'm your obligation!" His face was mottled with anger.

"You are one obligation, that's true. And I'm willing to go inside and discuss your anger with me—for the full session, if you like. But I hope it won't take that much time, so that we can discuss who else and what else you're angry with.''

That seemed to work. Jack's cheeks began to lose the bright red flush that made me wonder about his blood pressure. If he hadn't calmed down, I had been prepared to insist that we hold the session on the porch. I wasn't letting anyone in the grip of rage into my house. Even if it meant losing the client.

"Okay," Jack said. "And you're right. It isn't just you. I got here on time, ready to talk to you about Linda, and then I had to fucking sit on the fucking porch.''

''I can understand how frustrating that must have been,'' I assured him. ''Now let's go in and settle down, and you can tell me about Linda.''

Jack followed me into the house and settled down into the armchair I used for clients.

''You know what you suggested about listening to her?'' he said, almost before I was seated. ''I did. And I don't like her. Not just what I hear, I don't like her.''

''What is it that you don't like about her?''

Jack recited a list of Linda's failures, and I listened, kept on listening as he segued into how they reminded him of his mother's failures.

To appease him—and expiate my guilt—I gave him another ten minutes. Once he was safely out the door, I checked my answering machine.

''Fay, honey, it's Dixie. I just called to say how glad I am that you're joining us for dinner tomorrow night, and so is Evan. I can't tell you how thrilled we both are that you and Kirby are back together. See you tomorrow.''

I shut my eyes, squeezing them to keep from crying.

Maybe Dixie and I were predestined to continually disappoint one another.

Getting out of the house, taking a break before my next client arrived, suddenly seemed like a good idea.

Norman was the most likely witness to have seen Jorge and reported him to the police. Norman had called the police about the party, and he might have been watching for them when Jorge was in the street. But Norman worked Friday afternoon at an antiques and collectibles store, so I couldn't talk to him until later.

Ramon wouldn't be the witness. I had discovered at the end of the meeting, when everyone had signed a sheet of paper with name and address, that he actually lived next door to the Carrascos, to the south, and he wasn't related. He would have talked to them, however, not the police.

Sybil lived too far up the street, and the angle from Christopher's window was wrong. That left Carol, Frieda and Martine, and Marcus and his friends.

Frieda looked out of her window a lot. And older people sometimes are up late. And she lived next door to the Carrascos on the north. I decided to start with Frieda.

I crossed the street, carefully avoiding the dark splotch where the body had been, and knocked on the door of the white frame house.

Martine answered, wearing a faded, flowery housedress and a string of pearls with knots between each bead. I wondered how long she had had the pearls. And I hoped she kept them in a safe place when she wasn't wearing them.

"Come in, Faith," she said, nodding her head to show pink scalp covered with pale brown fuzz, an unsuccessful attempt to wash the gray away. "I'll make tea."

"I don't want to put you—"

"No, no. Come in."

Martine led me up a flight of stairs to a bedsitting room where Frieda sat in a rocking chair, staring out the window. Like Martine's pearls, the art on the walls and the Oriental carpet on the floor looked real. And expensive. The only furnishings other than Frieda's rocker were a four-poster bed and a small, carved table with two chairs beside it. The chairs had round, tapestried backs and no arms.

"Frieda!" Martine shouted. "I'm making tea!"

Frieda jumped, then reached up to touch her hearing aid. She motioned me toward one of the chairs.

"How are you?" I enunciated carefully, not wanting to shout at her.

"Fine. Tired."

Her face was end-of-the-line tired, the bones of her skull prominent under fine, sagging skin, and through tightly knotted white hair. Her eyelids were even starting to sag away from her pale brown eyes, showing barely pink rims. She rocked gently, clutching the arms of her quilted bathrobe, an ivory that might once have been white.

"Frieda, you said the other night that you've lived here a long time," I said. Under other circumstances, I wouldn't have leapt right in to the reason for my visit. But I didn't want to find my four o'clock waiting on the porch.

"Yah, a long time."

"Do you know the Carrascos well?"

"Who?"

"The Carrascos. They live next door. Esteban was

at the meeting Tuesday, the man with the white mustache.''

"Oh, the nice Mexican family."

I didn't correct her.

"I see them," Frieda continued. "They've lived in that house for years. I've watched the boy grow up."

"It's the boy I want to ask you about. The police arrested the boy, Jorge, and charged him with the murder that happened in the street last Friday night."

"Terrible. His mother must be so upset." Frieda shook her head.

"She is. She talked to me about it."

Martine bustled into the room with a silver tea service, placing it on the table in front of me.

"Martine, did you know?" Frieda asked.

"What?" Martine pulled the other straight chair up to the table.

"That nice boy from next door was arrested for murder."

"Why would he murder somebody? Such a shame. Lemon or cream?"

"Lemon, thank you," I said, picking up a bone china cup as translucent as Frieda's skin. "We don't know yet that he murdered somebody. Only that he was arrested."

"Why would the police arrest him if he didn't do it? Have a cookie, they're good, they're from the bakery on Sunset."

"Thank you." I took one to be polite, although I didn't particularly like sugar cookies. "The police think he did it, but they could be wrong."

"Yah," Frieda nodded. "Police make mistakes sometimes. Did you talk to the nice policeman who came to the meeting?"

"Yes. He was the one who made the arrest."

"What did he say?"

"He says someone saw Jorge with the knife in his hand."

Frieda looked out the window, shaking her head. "What a shame, what a terrible world."

I followed her gaze. The street was quiet, a few cars, no people. Amy was sitting on my porch, looking up as if she knew where I was. Mac was next to his mother, watching a squirrel run up the gingko tree. It didn't appear to be a terrible world. Except for the fresh graffiti on my garage door, and on Norman's garage door. I should take my turn with the paint brush.

"It's possible the witness made a mistake," I said. "I'd like to find out who saw Jorge. You can see so much from this window. I thought maybe you could help me."

"Not at night, no," Frieda said, shaking her head again. "I cannot see much at night. And I turn off my hearing aid, so I don't hear."

"Martine, you weren't by any chance looking out the window Friday, were you?"

"No, my bedroom is in the back, so I never know what is going on in the street. Only Frieda knows." Her mouth tightened as she said it.

"I will watch, Faith," Frieda said. "I'll let you know if I see anything that would help the boy or his poor mother."

I finished my cookie, drank a little tea, and explained that I had a client coming. Martine showed me to the door.

"She sleeps a lot," Martine said. "Once she turns off her hearing aid, she falls asleep."

"Let me know if you see or hear anything," I said. "And thank you for the tea."

My four o'clock appointment was just getting out of her car. I dashed across the street to meet her.

The four o'clock appointment segued into the five o'clock and the six o'clock. By seven, I was tired, ready to pack it in for the day. But as I waved goodbye to my last client, I saw Carol standing on her porch.

And Carol waved back.

I trotted across the street again.

"Want a beer?" Carol asked, holding up her own can.

"No, thanks. If you don't mind, I just wanted to ask a couple of questions."

"Go ahead."

I told the story, ending with the question about Friday night.

"Lisa—my roommate—and I were out," Carol said. "The cops were winding down the scene when we got home. I'm sorry I can't help."

"Well—do you by any chance know the Asian family?" I pointed to the house of the woman who had peered out the window when I was delivering flyers.

"The Hsiehs," Carol said. "Not well, but the daughter is in one of my classes."

"What do you teach?"

"Phys Ed at Madison High."

"Ah. Then maybe you could enlist the daughter's help."

Carol laughed. I could imagine her as a gym teacher, with her towel-dry short hair, her skin slightly dry from too many shower rooms and windy fields. And no makeup. For some reason, gym teachers never wore makeup.

"I'll talk to Eunice next time I see her. How's that?"

"That'll do," I said. "Thanks."

When I turned to cross back to my own house, I saw the lights coming on in Alex and Wayne's living room. The sun hadn't quite set. The day had been hazy, and the clouds still had a rosy tinge. I decided to talk to the two men before quitting for the night.

"Come in, come in," Wayne said when he answered my knock, waving a clinking glass. "What would you like to drink?"

I had turned down Carol's offer, but turning down Wayne's seemed unneighborly, especially when he and Alex were hosting the meetings.

Asking for wine was probably not a good idea with Alex and Wayne—anything they had on hand surely had a plastic top—and I didn't want anything hard.

"I'll take a beer," I said. Next time I would have a beer with Carol. I did want to get to know her.

Alex was sitting on the couch with his feet on the coffee table, Jack Daniels in one hand, lit cigarette in the other. I took the chair near the window. The air in the room was heavy with dancing particles from the overflowing ashtray.

On the television set, Vanna was turning the letters.

"Could we turn the volume down just a little?" I asked.

"Of course," Alex said. "It's up because I've been going back and forth from the kitchen. I've been fixing a special gumbo for Wayne. He works so hard, every once in a while I like to do something special for dinner."

"What a nice thing to do," I said, wondering one more time why Wayne would be willing to support a healthy adult, male or female, who did nothing all day but watch television, shop, and cook, without even keeping the house clean.

Wayne returned from the kitchen and handed me a Miller Lite.

"I should have brought you a glass," he said.

"The bottle's fine."

Wayne joined Alex on the couch. "What's going on?"

"Listen, guys, I want to talk with you about the murder last Friday night." I said it loudly, talking over the whirring Wheel.

Wayne picked up the remote and hit the mute button.

"Do the police know anything?" he asked.

"They've arrested somebody."

"Great!" Wayne said.

Alex picked up the remote.

"Not so great. They arrested Jorge Carrasco." I said it quickly, holding a hand toward Alex, hoping to forestall the release of the mute.

"So? Who's he?" Alex waved the remote.

"The son of Esteban, the man who was here on Tuesday, the one with the white mustache. And I'm not convinced Jorge did it. Neither is his attorney. This is a question of rights, Alex." It was a cheap shot, but I had to try it.

"If the beaner kid didn't do that, he did something else," Alex said. "Did the police have a reason to arrest him?"

"Sort of," I said. "They say they have a witness."

"That does it then," Wayne said. "They've got him."

"Maybe. I don't suppose either of you saw anything that night."

"Last Friday night? There was a special call-in program about AIDS on cable," Alex said. "We watched for hours. I fell asleep about midnight, and Wayne was still watching."

"I watched the whole thing," Wayne said. "God, it was scary."

That was the end of the Jorge Carrasco discussion. I listened to stories about dead and dying friends until I finished my beer and left.

Norman and Helena had fastened their shutters for the night. If the shutters had been fastened the week before, they wouldn't have seen anything. I could talk to them another time.

Marcus and Louie, too.

Friday night. The week was gone, a full Saturday was coming up, and I was tired.

Jorge Carrasco would have to wait.

SEVEN

THE DOORBELL RANG a little after nine the next morning.

My first client wasn't due until ten. I had fixed myself a latte, but I wasn't dressed or made up, and I wasn't anxious to see anyone.

But when I looked out the window and saw Graciela Carrasco, pink and white sweater vibrating in the morning sun, I opened the door.

"So how do I get him out?" she asked.

"This isn't a good time for me to talk," I said. "I have a client coming soon."

"I have a boy in jail. There is no good time for me to talk."

"You're right, and I'm sorry." I stood my ground in the doorway. I wasn't asking her in. "I don't have much to tell you. It's a difficult situation. The police say they have a witness, someone who saw Jorge do it."

"I know that, but they're wrong. He didn't do it. Didn't you tell them that?"

"Well, sort of, but it isn't that simple. I talked to Jorge's attorney, and—"

"That girl? You talked to that girl who calls herself Jorge's lawyer? Oh, God, who's going to pay any attention to her? What am I going to do?'' Graciela had her hand on her breast, gasping for breath.

I decided the woman wasn't going to faint.

"Miriam Stern seems competent to me,'' I said. "I'm certain she'll do fine. She believes in Jorge, and that's important.''

"Yeah, sure. But men won't listen to her. He ought to have a man for a lawyer. What did she tell you?''

"She doesn't know yet who the witness is, and she'd like to find out as quickly as possible, giving her time before the trial. I've been asking people on the block, but so far haven't found anyone who saw anything.''

"Okay. But you'll find out, right? You and that girl attorney? So I can get Jorge out of jail? A flight risk. The judge said he was a flight risk. Where would he go?''

"I understand your distress.'' I was doing my best to be patient. "I'm sure Miriam Stern would get bail if—''

"That's what I mean. Nobody pays attention to her.''

"I paid attention to her.''

"You're a woman. The judge will be a man.''

"You don't know that. And even if he is—'' I had had enough. "Graciela. I have a client coming. I cannot talk with you any longer, not now. I'll do the best I can, when I have time, to find out who the witness is. And so will Miriam Stern. And she'll defend Jorge as well as anyone would. I'm certain of that. I'll get back to you when I know something.''

Graciela gave me a look that would have inspired guilt in a sociopath. I met her eyes without flinching.

"Okay,'' she said. "You get back to me.''

I watched the woman move heavily down the steps, shoulders slumped. I shut the door, guilty but relieved.

I had left an hour break between my morning and afternoon appointments. I could use that time to talk with Marcus and Louie.

The music that marked the beginning and end of Marcus's waking hours came on about halfway through my eleven o'clock appointment. It was always loud enough to hear, rarely loud enough to bother me or my clients.

This particular client—a woman in the throes of career change, something I truly understood—didn't even notice.

Just before noon, I saw my eleven o'clock to the door and then cut across the gazania to Marcus's kitchen. The music got louder as I approached the house, and I had to pound to get attention.

"Come in, precious," Louie said. "Did you bring me a latte?"

"No. And I have clients all afternoon, so I can't invite you over." I was going to have to present Louie with his own mini-espresso maker some day. He came over two or three mornings a week to use mine. "Is Marcus up yet?"

"I think so. Come on in."

Marcus appeared over Louie's shoulder.

"Hey, baby," he said, moving Louie smoothly out of the way. "Give me a kiss."

I pecked the air next to his cheek.

"I have to talk to you about the murder," I said.

"What can we say? We never know when death will rise up and startle us. In the midst of life and all that."

I couldn't tell how serious he was, but he wasn't smiling.

"The boy who lives across the street, Jorge Carrasco, has been arrested. His mother and his attorney think he's innocent. So do I."

Marcus nodded. "Could be he is."

"But there's supposed to be a witness who went to the police. Could someone who was at the party have seen something and gone to the police about it?"

"I have to think. I have to think, first, who was here, and second, who might talk to the police."

"It would have to be someone who had been here before, too, someone who could identify Jorge, who knew where he lived. What about Denise?"

Marcus laughed. "I don't think so. But I'll ask her."

"Could have been somebody passing by," Louie said.

"Which reminds me. Have you ever told the police about the strange man asking directions at three a.m.?"

"What for? Wasn't the night of the murder, and they won't do nothing about it."

"It's just that they should know," I said. "With burglaries and murder and everything."

Louie shrugged.

"Not too many people we know talk to the police," Marcus said. "But I'll think about who might. You gonna be home this weekend?"

"Most of it. I'll be out tonight."

Marcus smiled and winked one of his bedroom eyes. "You have a good time, and I'll talk with you soon."

I bit my tongue to keep from blurting that I would be having dinner with Kirby and his parents. The news would only encourage misapprehension on Marcus's part.

I left, blushing.

I was about to go back inside and put something

together for a quick lunch when I saw Norman painting over graffiti on the garage doors. I trotted down the stairs to the street.

"That really is nice of you," I said. "I'd be happy to take turns with the paint brush."

"It doesn't take long," he replied. "It's easier just to do it."

"I wanted to ask—the night of the murder, after you called the police about Marcus's party—were you watching the street?"

"No. We had closed the shutters, and at least they blocked out a little of the racket. Why?"

I explained about the arrest and the witness.

"I can't help you," he said. "All I know about the Carrascos is that they don't make noise."

"Okay. And thanks again."

That did it for the street. Unless Marcus came up with somebody, or Carol got some information from Eunice Hsieh, there was no sign of a witness.

My afternoon appointments passed without incident. At five, I was left with what I hoped would be my last dilemma of the day—what to wear to dinner with the McKenzies.

I wanted to look glamorous, as if I truly belonged with the McKenzies, just this one time. And I knew Dixie would outshine me, no matter what I chose to wear. On top of that, the longer I worked at home, the less attractive I felt, partly because of the weight gain, partly because I was simply out of the glamour habit.

After three complete changes, I opted for what I hoped was understated yet effective. A royal blue silk dress, onyx and silver jewelry, black lace pantyhose, strappy black high heeled sandals.

Surely Dixie would approve. Next to Dixie, I would

look like somebody's wife. Like Phyllis, in fact. Phyllis and I had never cared for each other. But I could stand one more evening with Phyllis.

By the time I was ready, I was already half an hour late to meet Kirby, which wouldn't give us much time to talk. Les Etoiles was on the Westside, and we would have to leave forty-five minutes for travel time.

Kirby seemed startled when he opened the door, almost surprised to see me. He recovered quickly and held out his arms. I had a sinking feeling that whatever he had been doing while he waited had caused him to lose track of time.

"Hello, baby darling," he said, kissing me gently on the cheek. He had aimed for my lips, but I averted my head.

He was dressed so casually, in the same sport coat and slacks he had worn to Marcus's party, that I wished I had dressed down.

"Hi." I didn't shrug his arms off. I didn't hug back, either.

"Come in. What do you want? Wine? Do you want wine?"

"We'll have wine when we get there, and I don't want to start now. We may not eat for a couple of hours."

"That wouldn't have bothered you fifteen years ago."

"It does now."

He regarded me through narrowed eyes. "You don't mind if I have a glass, do you?"

I thought of all the answers I could give. "Do what you want."

His shoulders and hands were twitching as he walked to the kitchen, not a lot, but enough to suggest that he had already done a little blow. I hoped it was only a little.

He came back in a moment with a glass in his hand.

"Here's looking at you, kid," he said in his best Bogie voice. He took a sip, then stuck two fingers in the glass, wiped his nostrils with them, and sniffed. "How've you been? Are you fully recovered?"

"Yes. But it took almost two days. And I can't afford to get wasted like that anymore."

"Your therapy practice," he said, damning it with his tone.

"Yes, that. It may not be important to you, but it is to me. And then the last two days I've been running around talking to neighbors. The police arrested a boy who lives across the street for that murder, and I've been looking for a phantom witness to the crime."

"Oh, God, Fay, you're not."

"Yes, I am." I had almost forgotten how controlling he was. This time he wouldn't get to me.

"What part are you playing this time? Kinsey Milhone?"

"Cut it out, Kirby. I'm just trying to do a favor for the boy's mother. His attorney thought it would be easier to use me than an investigator, because I live there and some of them trust me."

He swirled the liquid in his glass, sniffed again.

"Maybe we better go," he said. "I don't want to be late for Evan's dinner."

"Okay." I almost offered to drive. But in a pinch, if he got too drunk, I could get Chas and Phyllis to drive me home.

I didn't like the way he pulled the Jaguar out of the garage or the way he sped down the hill. But it was too late to take my own car.

He glanced over in time to catch me flinch as he cut in front of a Buick to make the freeway entrance, and we rode the rest of the way in silence.

Les Etoiles was in Santa Monica, on Main Street, about three blocks from the beach. That section of Main Street was a sort of Rodeo Drive West, with cute little boutiques that charged outrageous prices for well-cut clothes with simple lines, garish boutiques that charged outrageous prices for clothes that no one over eighteen should wear, art galleries featuring the scribble-and-drip school, and a dozen restaurants ranging from pizzerias to sushi to postmodern Chinese to Les Etoiles. All were good, all were expensive. Dinner for two, with wine, would cost as much as everything I was wearing.

The requisite Silver Corniche was parked in front of the door. Kirby's Jaguar might rate a spot on the street on a slow night, but not on a Saturday. The valet drove it away somewhere.

Kirby and I entered the restaurant through a high purple arch with something embedded in the masonry that made it glitter. A starry night. There were large windows on either side, so that those not blessed with the price of admission could watch the chosen few, the diners.

Dixie and Evan were waiting at the bar.

"Fay! Kirby!" Dixie called, parting the crowd with her voice to let us through.

Dixie hugged, and I hugged back, at the moment truly glad to see her.

Her costume was even more extravagant than I had expected. She was wearing a silver and black chiffon dress straight from the flapper era, with a matching headband. Dixie was short and slender, but costumes gave her stature. Her hair was still partly brown and partly gray, frizzing wildly about her head. Her eyes were black star sapphires, sparkling in her lined, smiling face. Unlike most stars of her generation, Dixie had chosen to let her age show. And was all the more beautiful because of it.

Evan lumbered forward, embracing me clumsily with one arm to protect the glass in his other hand. He had aged less well. His long, elegant face was starting to sink, his hair, though full, was totally white. For the first time, I saw clouds in his blue eyes. He was wearing a tailored Western suit and a bolo tie held with a huge turquoise embedded in silver. Evan had affected Western wear ever since his television days as *Nevada Smith*. And with his height, and his broad shoulders, it seemed appropriate.

I kissed him on the cheek. He tried to kiss me back on the mouth, but I didn't let him reach it. His kisses had never been exactly fatherly. That had always seemed to be all right with Dixie, even if I wasn't quite comfortable with the display.

"I'll see about our table," Dixie said. "Chas and Phyllis should be here any moment."

"I'm glad to see you, Fay," Evan said.

"I'm glad to see you, too. Happy birthday."

"I suppose we're going to do that all night!" Kirby snapped.

"What?" I asked.

"Never mind." Kirby glared at Evan, who seemed puzzled.

"Come on, everybody," Dixie called from the maitre d's stand. Chas and Phyllis were next to her.

That was one of the things I admired about Dixie—

her ability to get people to do what she wanted, including in this case getting a maitre d' at a crowded restaurant to honor reservations on time. And she did it graciously, too.

"I'll be right back," Kirby said.

I held Evan's arm as we maneuvered our way through to the table. The restaurant seemed built like an amphitheater, so that conversations were magnified, not hushed. I didn't understand the appeal, unless the regular clientele had scarred eardrums from too many rock concerts, and memories of a time when it had to be loud to be real. Or unless they all wanted to be spared any attempt at serious discussion.

Kirby was a little less jittery but a little wilder-eyed when he returned from the men's room.

Dixie had seated me on Evan's right, next to Chas, who was an older, slimmer, red-gold version of Kirby, without the beard. Kirby without the excesses. Chas was a poet who had chosen an academic life, figuring that the university was the safest place for poets in this world. Chas was wrong, of course—there is no safe place for poets, anywhere—but I liked Chas anyway.

Kirby sat across from Chas, on his mother's right, next to Phyllis. Phyllis looked just as she had fifteen years earlier—like a displaced farm girl in need of a makeover. She was wearing a pink-and-maroon flowered dress that would have looked retro chic on someone else but looked dowdy on her.

I didn't think academic wives were required to be dowdy. But it occurred to me that camouflage might be the secret of Chas and Phyllis's marriage. Phyllis could discreetly play the academic games that Chas had no head for, attracting no attention as she did it. Creating the safe place that Chas had wanted. Otherwise, the lasting relationship made no sense to me. I could not fantasize how they had ever connected, although I had tried more than once when I was living with Kirby.

Phyllis smiled tightly, aware of my scrutiny.

Ordering took time, since the young waiter had to recite the specials three times over the din, and Phyllis didn't want any of the specials, so she had to look at the menu, and Kirby couldn't decide what to order because he clearly wasn't hungry.

"How've you been, Chas?" I asked quietly, talking under the noise. "Deconstructionists getting you down?"

Chas laughed. "They run the department, but I think I'll survive."

"I saw that profile in the *Times* when your collected poems came out last year. I'm impressed."

"Write enough for long enough and somebody collects you," Chas said.

"Only if you're good," I answered.

"I want to hear about you, Fay," Dixie said loudly, leaning across him.

"There's not much to tell. I lead a quiet life." I smiled, hoping Dixie wouldn't urge me to reveal intimacies at the top of my lungs.

"She says that, oh, yes, but it's not true. She's on the trail of a murderer!" Kirby was smiling, his eyes gleaming.

"What?" Dixie was startled.

"It's nothing," I said quickly, sorry I had mentioned it to Kirby. "I'm doing a favor for an attorney and a neighbor's son, who's been accused of a murder. It's no big deal."

"Why, of course it is," Dixie said. "Community

involvement is very important. I don't know what's got into Kirby tonight.''

"Dixie, what about you?" I asked. "I read that you and Evan are going to be doing a revival of *Touch of the Poet* in Pasadena."

Dixie took over center stage and talked through dinner, ignoring Kirby, who was able to push his food around and pretend to eat. I had trouble ignoring him, but I managed to enjoy the endive and watercress salad and the grilled scallops with papaya salsa anyway.

I had only taken one sip of my cappuccino when Kirby said, "Let's go."

Under other circumstances, I would have argued for the rest of my coffee. But getting Kirby out of the restaurant while he was still more or less under control was without doubt a good idea.

I said goodbye to everyone with much hugging and kissing, hearing promises of getting together soon without returning them. I could call Dixie in a day or two and explain.

Kirby shifted restlessly from one foot to the other while we waited for his Jaguar. I thought again about offering to drive, but I decided he could make it home.

I held onto my seatbelt as we sped in silence back to the Santa Monica Freeway, to the Harbor Freeway, to the Golden State Freeway, to the Los Feliz exit, to his house.

He hit the automatic garage door opener, pulled in, and turned the engine off.

"I'm sorry," he said. "I know that wasn't much fun for you."

"I enjoyed seeing Evan and Dixie," I answered. "Do you want to tell me what's wrong?"

"No. But I'd like it if you came in for a while."

Kirby said it without his usual dramatic presentation. I nodded and followed him out of the garage. I hadn't yet told him that I couldn't see him again, and I still meant to do that. I had to do that. And maybe I could point out to him that he was hurting himself, and he didn't need to. He was so talented, surely he must know that he didn't need to hurt himself, that he could get help.

Kirby was staring at a small mass huddled on the porch when I reached the bottom of the stairs.

"Tigger?"

The small mass didn't move.

"Tigger? Come on, man."

Kirby leaned down to shake him. Tigger fell off the steps. And he still didn't respond.

"Tigger?"

EIGHT

"CALL THE POLICE," I said. My voice was low and calm and sounded as if it were coming from someone else. I began to shiver, even though the evening was still warm. "We have to call the police."

"No, come on, help me get him to the car. We'll take him to the hospital."

Kirby had tried frantically to rouse Tigger—slapped him, shaken him, breathed into his mouth—and it hadn't done any good. I had tried both his neck and his wrist for a pulse. Nothing.

Kirby was struggling to lift the body, get him to his feet, but that wouldn't do any good either.

"He's dead, Kirby," I said. "Leave him there, open the door, and I'll call the police."

"Oh, God, no."

Kirby sat down heavily on the step, still holding Tigger's body, rocking it. He started to cry, deep, wrenching sobs. I sat down next to him, reaching out, rocking with the two of them.

"Hush, now," I said. "Hush, now, it'll be all right."

I didn't believe that, but as I kept repeating it, Kirby quieted down. I brushed the hair off his forehead.

"I need the keys," I said.

"I think I dropped them," he whispered.

The keys had landed just out of the bright circle from

the porchlight, still close enough for a reflected glimmer. The second one I tried turned the deadbolt.

Kirby had left the lights on in the music room. A cordless phone was sitting on the piano bench. I picked it up and punched 911.

I waited while it rang, then explained the situation to the operator, giving the address and the phone number, and all the information I had on Tigger, which wasn't much. Wasn't enough.

"I'll send the paramedics," the operator said, "although a dead body isn't strictly a life-threatening emergency, unless you believe that there was violence involved, and the perpetrator may still be in the vicinity. You might want to have the dispatcher's number handy, for use in non-emergency situations."

I disconnected her before she could give me the number.

Kirby was carefully arranging Tigger's body on the steps when I returned to the porch.

"I have to check the house," he said. "The cops may want to come in."

He moved away from the body and stumbled on the doorsill. I tried to catch him, but he caught himself against the jamb. I thought he was going to start crying again, but he turned and straightened, and cleared his eyes with the heels of his hands.

"What am I going to do?" he asked, less of me than the door or the night.

"Check the house," I said firmly, reducing the question from the existential level to the immediate, material one.

Part of me wanted him to break down in front of the police. If he were busted for possession, detox and community service would be the sentence, given his celebrity, and it would probably be the best thing that could happen to him. But not through me. I couldn't turn him in. The part of me that wanted to protect him from consequences won.

"Right now, you have to check the house."

I took his hand and walked him inside.

While Kirby wandered through the dining room, kitchen, and downstairs bedroom and bathroom, I cleaned out ashtrays and looked for anything that might bring to mind drugs. I couldn't smell any marijuana residue once the ashtrays were dumped, and I decided against spraying with air freshener. Too suspicious.

When two police officers suddenly materialized next to the couch, I realized that the front door was still open. I introduced myself and called out for Kirby.

Whatever he had taken in the bathroom had left him cool enough to deal with the police. He told the officers what had happened, that the two of us had had dinner with his parents—he mentioned names, and the officer taking notes nodded—and had found Tigger on the steps when we returned. He put his arm around me, and I smiled at the officers. I told them who I was and where I lived.

"Fay was on the *Coffee Break* show," Kirby prompted. "And she was on *Saints and Sinners,* too."

"My wife watches that," the officer taking notes said. "I'll tell her I met you."

"Not for years," I blurted, surprised that Kirby could come up with the names of the shows. "I haven't been on either one for years."

The officer nodded.

Kirby confirmed that Tigger lived at the address on his driver's license, which was in his wallet. His real name was Andrew Smith.

The paramedics had loaded Tigger into the ambulance while the officers talked to Kirby and me. The second officer volunteered that they hadn't found any signs of violence.

The first officer politely told Kirby that they might have to get in touch with him after the autopsy.

Then the officers left.

The room was empty and cavernous.

Kirby stood there looking at the closed door.

"I have to call Gordo and Ray," he said.

He picked up the cordless phone from the piano and took it into the bedroom. I could hear the muffled sounds of his voice.

I was still standing somewhere between the piano and the sofa when the front door opened and Gordo walked in, pale, hollow-eyed, and stunned. I told him the little I knew.

When Kirby came back, he went directly to the piano, not looking at either of us.

"Maybe we could play for Tigger," he said.

Gordo nodded and picked up his horn.

"Got any toot?" Gordo asked.

Kirby held out a small glass vial.

Gordo helped himself and held it out to me.

I clenched my fists to keep them at my side and shook my head. I watched the cocaine pass from Gordo's hand to Kirby's, then back to Kirby's pocket, holding my breath the whole time.

Kirby's hands hit the keys, a minor chord, and Gordo's horn burst out a low wail.

I waited a moment, then slipped out the front door, leaving them to their pain. Once outside, I began to breathe again.

I was glad home was close, because I wasn't certain

how far I could drive. Even though I hadn't know Tigger, I felt diminished by his death. The John Donne syndrome.

Amy and Mac were waiting on the porch. I opened the door, and they trotted in ahead of me. I shed my clothes, washed the makeup off my face, and crawled into bed, clutching Mac as if he were a teddy bear. He struggled until I loosened my grip, then began to purr, deep, contented purrs that normally would have eased me into sleep.

But my muscles had ossified. And the nerve endings in the bottom of my feet were tingling. Relaxation would not come.

I mentally ran through the contents of my bathroom cabinet, wishing that something in there would help me sleep, knowing that the prescription narcotics had gone at the same time the nonprescription ones had, years ago.

I understood how it could happen, how Kirby could escape into drugs and music, and I would not go back to that. Kirby was not the Man for my Island. Or at least not any longer. Whatever else the years had done, it had brought me the knowledge that all we were to each other were separate islands, floating in a wide ocean.

I fell asleep sometime, because it was light when the telephone rang, waking me up. Amy and Mac had pinned me down, and I had to push them both away to get to the phone.

After a fuzzy exchange of hellos, I realized I was talking to Martine.

"You asked about what I saw or heard," Martine said. "I don't know for certain, but I might have heard the motorcycle. I don't remember which nights I heard him, but I heard him last night. The boy on the motorcycle, he comes home all the time in the middle of the night and wakes me up."

"Who are you talking about? What boy on a motorcycle?" I asked.

"You maybe sleep through, but I wake up, all the time, every night he comes home late. I don't see him so much during the day, but I think he lives in the apartment building at the end of the block. Just look for the motorcycle."

I thanked her and hung up. I had heard a motorcycle from time to time, although it didn't wake me up at night. But if it was loud enough to wake Martine, it would surely have bothered Norman. I would ask him.

Sunday morning. I was supposed to do something on Sunday morning. I had fixed a latte and brought in the *Times* from the porch before I remembered that I was having brunch with Michael.

A friend is a bridge to the mainland.

Showering and dressing helped to reestablish the link.

And acting on Martine's information might help, too.

Norman's windows were unshuttered, and noises were coming from his kitchen. I cut over to his house and rapped on the windowsill.

A knife clattered to the floor.

"What?" he called.

"I'm sorry," I said. "I didn't mean to startle you. But do you know anything about the guy with the motorcycle?"

"I know he lives in the apartment building at the end of the block, but that's all," Norman said stiffly. "I don't know which number. Why?"

"I thought he might be the witness to the murder."

"He comes home late enough."

"Thanks."

I headed down Norman's stairs and crossed back to my garage. I could look for the motorcyclist after brunch.

I had agreed to meet Michael at a small cafe on Santa Monica Boulevard, not far from his Kings Road condo. There were a few outdoor tables, with black umbrellas leaning over the sidewalk, in a cramped area smelling of car exhaust and cigarette smoke. Michael was already seated at one, nibbling a small cheese Danish taken from a basket containing an assortment of breads.

"Two blocks," I grumbled as I sat down. "I had to park two blocks away."

"And you probably passed four spaces that you didn't want to maneuver into," Michael said.

"Or driveways I didn't want to obstruct. Why are we outside with the smokers?"

"Because the inside is too crowded for conversation. And there were so many laptops on the tables that I thought I had wandered into a screenwriters' convention." Michael waved at the waiter, who nodded. "I told him to rush a latte when you arrived. How are you?"

"Fine, sort of. How are you?"

"Terrific. Elizabeth's agent was able to leverage the possible perfume interest into a new commitment from Pretty Kitty cat food. What does the 'sort of' mean?"

"It means I had dinner with the McKenzies last night, and a friend of Kirby's was lying dead on the porch when we got back to his place."

Michael checked my eyes, frowning.

"Stop that," I said.

"I'm only concerned for your emotional health, as any friend would be."

"No drugs. Last Wednesday was a slip, not a total relapse. And Kirby had enough for everyone. I left him playing the piano, not even aware I was gone."

The waiter, a young, attractive man with a wide smile and a surfer's tan, placed a latte in front of me.

"Ready to order?" he asked.

"What are you having?" I asked Michael.

"The ratatouille crepes and a glass of fresh orange juice," he answered.

"Fine. I'll have that, too." I smiled at the waiter.

The waiter smiled at Michael. "Coming right up."

Michael smiled back, then turned to me. "That's two violent deaths in just over a week. You seem to be holding up awfully well."

"I don't think Tigger's death was violent. Or not exactly. The autopsy will tell, but I'll be surprised if it's anything other than cocaine overdose, or cocaine and something else. And if I'm holding up well, it's only because I didn't know either of the people who died, and I have other things to distract me. My clients, for example. And that woman who wants me to help her son."

I tried the latte. It was a little weak, but otherwise all right. I picked a miniature bran muffin out of the basket.

"Anything new with the boy in jail?"

"His attorney asked me to help find the witness— she thinks the Neighborhood Watch gives me credibility. I have a possible lead, and I'll check it out this afternoon. Once I've found him, I think that's the end of it."

Michael frowned. "Then find another distraction. Did you tell Kirby you're not going to see him again?"

"I couldn't. It would have been kicking him when he was down. And I may have to see him, if there's some kind of intervention and I get subpoenaed. Besides, this may be the moment to intervene."

"It's a wonderful thought, Faith, but what makes you think he'll listen?"

"A dead friend could be the catalyst for change. And I'll enlist Dixie. If he won't listen to me, he'll listen to both of us. We got him to stay in school when he wanted to quit. We can get him to a rehab program."

Michael poked in the basket, then pulled out an apricot Danish. "I hope you're right. But I won't hold my breath. More than that. I hope trying to help Kirby doesn't hurt you."

"I know." I reached out and squeezed his hand.

"How are things going with your sole male client? Better, I hope."

I shook my head. "Worse. I was late meeting him Friday because of the attorney, and he was so angry that I considered all over again limiting my practice to women."

"If you think he may act out, you can refer him to someone else, you know that."

"You want him?"

"Absolutely not. Elizabeth's career demands my attention, and I'm not taking any new clients right now. Especially ones that may be borderline psychos."

"Oh, God, I hope he isn't that."

The smiling waiter deposited our plates, barely blinking as he took in the conversation.

"Anything else?"

I started to say no, but realized he wasn't asking me. Michael shook his head and picked up his fork.

"The waiter," I said. "That's why we're here."

"He's really an actor, of course. And I'm only thinking about it. I haven't done any more than chat with him."

"Be careful. Some things are more dangerous than drugs."

"I'm always careful. Elizabeth needs me." He said it around a mouthful of crepes.

I tried my own. The crepes were a little dry, but the vegetables had been grilled, and that made up for it. The fried potatoes had a perfect crunch, too. By the time I had cleared most of my plate and ordered a second latte, I was feeling better about life.

When Michael tried to pick up the check, I balked.

"My turn," I insisted.

"I know, but I think I might stay for another latte after you've left. If you don't mind."

"Not at all." I pushed my chair back enough to slide myself out of it, trying not to hit the young man at the next table. "Next time is on me, then."

Michael wiggled his fingers in assent.

I kissed his cheek and left.

The good thing about having to dash across Santa Monica Boulevard and then walk two blocks to my car was that I would burn calories. An exercise program, I promised myself, soon.

Santa Monica Boulevard curved into Sunset Boulevard only a few blocks from my house. I turned off Sunset, drove up the hill, and decided a little more walking was in order. I stopped just long enough to garage the car and drop off my purse.

The apartment house that Martine and Norman had

been talking about was at the end of the block and the top of the hill. The building and its grounds reminded me of Raymond Chandler and Hollywood in the thirties. A spiked, wrought iron fence covered with orange and magenta bougainvillea extended across the front of the property, with a double gate blocking the driveway to the parking area. White stucco flaked onto the lawn between languid pepper trees planted too close to the walls.

The gate wasn't locked, so I let myself in. The yard was larger than it seemed from the street. Overgrown roses dropped around an empty fountain, the dry pedestal for a chipped concrete Venus. There was something regally insouciant about her, even in her disrepair, and I had an urge to take her home and clean her up.

As I walked down the driveway, I discovered that there were actually four separate duplexes with narrow courtyards in between. I proceeded to the back of the complex, hoping to find marked parking spaces with a motorcycle in one.

And there it was, a midnight blue Harley sitting squarely in the middle of a space with 1B stenciled on the asphalt.

A crumbling concrete stairway with a wrought iron rail led up the side of the building nearest the street to the door marked 1B.

The man who answered my knock was wearing a faded gray flannel robe from which bare arms and bare legs protruded. His hair was an uncombed mass of brown losing the fight with gray, after having ceded what I could see of his beard, a three-day growth, long ago. His mouth was set in anger, and his eyes—a bright blue—were narrowed.

"What?" he growled.

"I'm sorry. I didn't mean to disturb you. But I'm not a Jehovah's Witness and I don't care that you're not in church, if that helps."

"So who are you?"

"A neighbor. Faith Cassidy. I live just down the block, in the small blue stucco house."

"And?"

He wasn't making this easy.

"Well—there was a murder on the street a week ago, and a young man has been arrested. His mother says he's innocent, and she asked me to help. His attorney thinks he may be innocent, too. She said there was a witness, and another neighbor thought you might be the witness, so I thought I'd drop by and ask you."

"Oh, God," he groaned. "You try to be a good citizen, and this is what you get."

I smiled brightly and waited.

He looked at me, and his face softened. He was almost handsome.

"Okay, Faith who is not a Jehovah's Witness," he said. "Come on in."

I followed him into a sunny room with hardwood floors and high ceilings, furnished with several large pillows and a few low tables. A canvas the size of a small mural sitting on an easel took up the entire center of the room. A combination of sheets and newspapers protected the floor for a foot in each direction.

"I suppose you want coffee," he said, slapping his bare feet against the floor.

"You don't have to go to any trouble," I said, hoping he would take it as a polite refusal. In fact, I didn't want coffee. I'd already had enough for the day.

"No problem." He padded toward the kitchen.

I moved forward to inspect the canvas. Faint pencil marks caught the rough outline of the Los Angeles panorama that danced beyond the open French windows. The apartment had an amazing view. To the right was Hollywood, the white houses and green trees climbing brown hills marked by the sign—H O L L Y W O O D—and the round dome of the Griffith Park observatory. To the left was flat white and green city with a few eruptions of steel gray towers, slowly fading toward the haze of the horizon.

Looking out the window, I felt a surge of love for L.A. that surprised and embarrassed me. A sense of being home.

I was still staring at the city when the man returned with two tall, earthenware mugs of what turned out to be Cuban cafe con leche.

"I'm Richard," he said. He had combed his hair and exchanged his robe for jeans and a faded *International Tribune* sweat shirt.

"Okay, Richard who is an artist," I answered. "I like your choice in coffee."

"Thanks." He gestured toward a pillow. "Have a seat and tell me what this is about."

"There's not much more I can say." I settled cross-legged onto a black pillow with a spray of cattleya orchids painted on it. I would have held the mug, but someone else had already stained a teak table that barely cleared the floor. I placed the mug carefully on the round stain. "I'd like to help the Carrascos if I can."

"Why you?" He sat on the other side of the table on a matching pillow.

"Because I was burglarized, so I organized a Neighborhood Watch, and his mother thinks that being block captain conferred some authority on me."

He nodded. "That's right. There was a flyer in my mailbox about the meeting. I thought about coming."

"Come next time. Anyway, the ADA who has the case has been playing games with Jorge Carrasco's attorney about the identity of the witness, hoping for a plea bargain. She thought I could help out by finding the witness, discovering exactly what he saw." I smiled expectantly.

"Okay—but it wasn't that much. I was coming home a week ago Friday a little after eleven—I hang out at the Blue Pearl a lot, they have poetry readings on Friday—and as I turned the corner, I caught this kid in my headlight, standing with a knife in his hand. As I zipped by, I saw a body on the ground. The kid holding the knife lives in the stucco house down the block that's kind of a dirty ochre. That's it."

"You're sure he had the knife in his hand?"

"Yeah, I'm sure."

"What did you do then?"

"I didn't want to take on a kid with a knife. I'm not into martial arts, and I'm not a hero. I came home, parked my bike, and called the police. I went downstairs to wait for them—staying carefully in the shadows—and I saw a black-and-white already turning the corner." He rubbed his shoulders, then his knees, as if remembering was hard for him. "I sat down for a minute to get my act together, and then the paramedics were there, and the street was swarming with people— I think I saw you—and I decided to wait until it all calmed down before I talked to the police again. They already had my name and number from the 911 call. I wasn't happy about any of this. Involvement with this kind of thing is not my style.''

"And that's it."

"That's right."

"Oh, hell. Jorge admitted being at the scene and touching the body. He said he couldn't remember touching the knife. You didn't see the act itself, did you?''

"No. I would have told you."

"Then his attorney's right. He shouldn't plea bargain. Especially since the knife was left in the body.''

"In the body?'' He frowned. "Great. There'll be a trial, and I'll lose days having to show up and sit in the courtroom while the attorneys play games.''

"Sorry. But it's going to help, knowing that the eyewitness may have doubts.''

Richard shook his head. "Help the kid, not the eyewitness. Why do you care?''

"I'm not really sure. But I am involved in this. Graciela Carrasco asked me to help when I was trying to nurture a seed of community spirit on a block, in a city, where the common good is an alien notion, and I didn't say no. If it helps, I've been trying to get out of it ever since.''

He ran his hands back through his hair and looked at me. "Faith. Is that really your name? Faith?''

"Yes.'' I didn't feel like explaining.

"Okay, Faith. What do you want with me?'' Humor lines crinkled around his eyes.

"Just tell what you saw to Jorge's attorney.''

I slapped down the notion that I might want something else. Except, of course, to see more of his work than the sketch on the canvas, but that could wait. I was feeling too vulnerable because of the mess with Kirby—the mess Kirby had become—and I was not in a mood to flirt.

"I'd better go." I finished my coffee and put the mug back on the low table.

"Okay." He let me reach the door before he added, "Hey, why don't we exchange phone numbers? Next time you want coffee, you can call me first."

I turned sharply, ready to snap at him, but he was smiling. So I waited while he found paper and pen, then exchanged numbers.

"An obligation goes with the number," I said. "Call me if you think of anything that might help Jorge."

"Ouch. Is it okay if I call for no reason at all?"

"It's okay."

I smiled back.

And I was still smiling, still holding his phone number in my hand as I retraced my way to the street. The smile faded when I reached home.

Graciela Carrasco was waiting on the steps.

NINE

"I JUST CAME from church," Graciela Carrasco said.

She was wearing a shiny black short-sleeved dress, tight enough to show the lines of her underwear and the bulge of flesh between bra and belt. Her black pumps looked painfully tight as well, edges cutting into her swollen arches.

The clusters of jet on her earlobes caught the light as she stood up. She tucked a black pocketbook under her arm and walked forward to meet me.

"I thought you might want to go with me to the jail," she continued, "to talk to Jorge, let him know you're working on this, that it's going to be okay. Okay?"

I thought of all the excuses I might give.

"Okay," I said. "Just let me grab my purse."

I had been willing to walk to the end of the block with only my keys, but I was not venturing near the County Jail without identification. Among the assholes with books I had interviewed on *Coffee Break* was a former state prison librarian who had been caught in a riot, sprayed with tear gas and foam, and forced to strip. He had started crying—on camera—as he described the terror he felt, stark naked, trying to prove his identity to a guard with a gun.

Stark naked it would be obvious that I didn't belong in a county jail segregated by sex. Nevertheless, I felt slightly uncomfortable even visiting. The discomfort was irrational, I knew that. I hadn't broken the law in years, not counting the evening I had spent with Kirby. And not counting habitual speeding. But old fears died hard, like bad habits.

When I returned with my purse, a large black leather bag that contained not only wallet, glasses, hairbrush, and makeup, but calendar and notebook as well, Graciela nodded.

"We'll take your car," she said.

I followed her to the garage, impressed with her tenacity. I hoped Jorge was worth what his mother was putting into him.

Graciela waited while I backed the Taurus out of the garage, got out, and pulled the heavy door shut. Once I was again behind the steering wheel, Graciela joined me, looking stoic.

I dropped down Marathon to Alvarado and turned left on Temple, skipping the freeway. Once we had passed the Music Center and the few other signs of civilization that downtown had to offer, we reached the jail. Graciela directed me to the visitor's parking lot.

The Los Angeles County Jail, with all the rest of the County Sheriff's facilities, was in an old stone building that seemed part of an earlier city that the big developers and redevelopers had worked hard to replace. A new jail had been built—the Twin Towers—but prisoners were still being held in the old one.

A wide marble staircase swept from a spacious rotunda to the second floor. A young man in a green jail uniform sat at a shoeshine stand near the foot of the stairs. No dull shoes for the deputies.

Graciela led me away from the stairs to an elevator, which we took to the third floor. The elevator opened into a small barred area, with a barred guard's cage to the right.

"I'll say you're his cousin," Graciela muttered. "That his father's sister is your mother. You and Jorge were very close when you were children, and it is important that you see him. That way you can come back without me."

"I think you should simply say that I'm his therapist."

"Jorge doesn't—"

"Besides, I'm already on some kind of list. His attorney thought I should visit."

"Okay. You are his therapist."

Graciela had a brief discussion with the deputy in the cage, then turned and motioned me forward. I signed in below Graciela on a clipboard pushed through a narrow opening in the cage. We picked up visitor's badges and fastened them to our clothes.

"You were right. That girl put you on some kind of list," Graciela said.

A guard appeared on the other side of the barred door. He reminded me of Broderick Crawford, or a bulldog. Or both. He glanced inside Graciela's purse, then stuck his hand in mine, glaring, as if he knew what I had thought. He led us down another paneled hall with hardwood floors. Then he opened a paneled door into a small room, and there the glamor stopped.

Suddenly the floors were cement and the walls white tile, like an old gym. There was a small table with two folding chairs.

"Go ahead, sit," Graciela said. "I want you to talk to him."

"Since I'm here as his therapist," I said, "I think you should wait outside."

Graciela opened her mouth and shut it. "Just let me see him, okay?"

"Okay." I sat in one of the chairs.

A moment later, a guard opened the door on the other side of the room and a young man in dark blue jail garb entered. The guard, who was young and black, shut the door and leaned against the wall.

"Jorge—" Graciela began, but I cut her off.

"Jorge, I'm Faith Cassidy, the therapist who lives across the street from your parents. Your attorney and your mother both think it might help if you talked to me."

Jorge looked from me to his mother and back.

"I know you," he said. "You drive the blue Taurus. And Miss Stern said you might stop by."

"She's gonna help," Graciela said.

"I'll try," I said. "And now your mother is going to leave us to talk."

Graciela glared at me.

"I'll see you later," she said to Jorge.

Graciela knocked on the door, and the older guard let her out.

Jorge smiled at me and settled casually into the other chair. I could understand why the police saw him as one more Hispanic kid gone wrong. His hair was short, almost shaved, along the sides of his head, but the top was long, curling down and around the nape of his neck. His eyelids hung at half-staff, and tobacco-stained teeth showed behind the smile. His left temple had turned deep purple from an abrasion.

"What happened to your head?" I asked.

"That depends on who you talk to, me or the cops," he answered, still smiling.

"I'm talking to you. I may ask the cops later."

"The two guys that came to arrest me—Page and

Davila, you know them?'' He paused, and I nodded. ''They were pretty nervous about the whole thing, like I was some kind of dangerous dude. And my mom got pretty upset, and she let fly some stuff in Spanish, and Davila answered her in Spanish, and I turned to tell her it was all right. Then Page grabbed my shoulder and spun me around, and I lost my balance. I guess I grabbed him as I fell, because we both ended up on the floor. Davila got scared and kicked me a couple of times, so I didn't put my arms down so they could cuff me, because I was protecting my head, and I got a little roughed up.''

''What's their story?''

''I threatened Page and they had to restrain me. I'm also charged with assault and battery on a policeman and resisting arrest, as well as murder.''

''Great. Just great. This gets better and better all the time. Now tell me about the murder.''

He shrugged, but he was still smiling. ''Are you really a therapist?''

''I'm really a therapist. I can invoke therapist-client confidentiality if that's what you want.''

''What I'm gonna say to you is just what I said to the police and the attorney. I didn't even see the murder. I was coming home from a party, and when I turned the corner, I saw this guy lying in the middle of the street. He was curled up on his side, and when I rolled him onto his back, I saw he was a homeboy with a knife sticking out of him. I parked the car and went in the house. I was going to call the cops, but then I looked out the window and saw the black-and-white. I had blood on my shirt, and I figured I wasn't going to be able to explain to them what happened. So I didn't try until they came to pick me up.''

Play The Lucky Hearts Game

and get...
FREE BOOKS & a FREE GIFT...
YOURS to KEEP!

Yes! I have scratched off the silver card. Please send me my **2 FREE BOOKS** and **FREE GIFT**. I understand that I am under no obligation to purchase any books as explained on the back of this card.

Scratch Here!
then look below to see what your cards get you...

415 WDL DH5S

NAME   (PLEASE PRINT CLEARLY)

ADDRESS

APT.#   CITY

STATE   ZIP

Twenty-one gets you
2 FREE BOOKS and
a **FREE GIFT!**

Twenty gets you
2 FREE BOOKS!

Nineteen gets you
1 FREE BOOK!

TRY AGAIN!

(ML-02/02) DETACH AND MAIL CARD TODAY!

He said it calmly and patiently. If he was lying, he was talented indeed.

"You know the police say they have a witness."

"Yeah, that's what my attorney said. How could they? Witness to what?"

"You didn't see anyone around?"

"No. Just a guy on a Harley. I think he lives somewhere at the end of the block."

In my best professional manner, I suppressed a surge of annoyance before Jorge could see it.

"Why didn't you tell your attorney about the guy on the Harley?" I asked calmly.

"Because he went roaring by, and he couldn't have seen my face. Besides, guys on Harleys don't usually volunteer anything to cops."

"Jorge, the guy on the Harley is the witness. He says you had the knife in your hand."

Jorge's eyelids went from half-staff to wide open. "He's wrong. I didn't. I may have touched the knife, I don't remember too clearly, but I never had it in my hand."

"And the knife wasn't yours."

"No."

"Are you a member of a gang?"

"No. But the cops don't want to believe that."

"Can you prove you aren't?"

He shrugged. "I don't know. I could probably get some teachers from the high school to say what a good guy I am, if you think that would help. How do you prove you're not a member of something?"

"It's tough, you're right. And character references from teachers might be a good idea." I wasn't quite ready to leave the night of the murder. "You said you were at a party. Why did you leave so early?"

"You mean why was I on my way home while that black dude's party was just getting going?"

"Something like that." I smiled at him.

"Because nothing was happening at the party, and I was tired. I have a job after school—or had a job—and I told my mother I would work in the yard on Saturday morning. My father had a heart attack last year, and he can't do much around the house anymore, so I do it."

"Tell me about the job."

"Nothing to tell. I drive a delivery truck for a grocery store."

"What store?"

"Nino's, on Sunset. Nino provides service, because he can't compete on price. A lot of old people in the neighborhood, people who don't like to walk, ask Nino for delivery."

"That's right. I've seen the truck." I had been watching for signs of discomfort, signs of evasion, signs of any kind that the young man might be trying to con me or mislead me. I hadn't seen any, and I hadn't felt any. Everything I picked up from the kid encouraged me to believe that he was being straightforward. "Let's talk about school. You said your teachers might be willing to talk about what a good guy you are. How are you doing in school?"

"I am an honor student. You can check."

I was surprised, and then embarrassed over my surprise.

"And English is your second language," I said.

"Yeah," he nodded, grinning. "Are you surprised I talk so good?"

I knew he was mocking me. I couldn't blame him.

"You do talk good. Tell me the story."

"I was born in Miami. My parents lived in an area

where they didn't have to speak anything but Spanish. When I was six, they finally gave up on the idea of ever getting back to Cuba, and we moved to Los Angeles. My mother didn't like what she heard about the public schools, so she put me in a Catholic school, and all they talked was English, and I would come home and cry because I couldn't understand anything. But she was taking English lessons at night, and we worked on the language together. By the time I was in third grade, I was getting A's in English. And almost everything else.''

I hoped Miriam Stern knew all that. Whatever America may think of itself, Los Angeles wasn't a melting pot, not in my experience. Someone had coined the term "tossed salad," but even that suggested the willingness to be part of the same dish. L.A. was more like buffets served from separate tables. All in the same room, but that was about it. Because the tables are separate, choices are made, stereotypes are created around the choices, and prejudice around the stereotypes.

I had expected Jorge, from his appearance, to be sitting at the Latino table, and I was uncomfortable realizing how quickly I had stereotyped him. And how quickly almost everyone I knew would have done the same. But Jorge's voice was telling me that he could eat from either table, Latino or Anglo. Not that it should matter. It depended on how he saw his future.

"What do you want to do when you get out of high school?" I asked.

"I think college, and then maybe law school."

"Just what the world needs. One more lawyer."

"I think the world could use one more bilingual public defender, don't you?"

"Okay. I'm impressed."

"Thanks. I hope it helps."

"That I'm impressed? I can't imagine how it might. But I will talk to Miriam Stern tomorrow and tell her what I've found out. Did you give her the names of teachers who might be willing to vouch for you?"

"Yes. I told her to talk to Mr. Zaslov, my English teacher, and Mr. Moreno, the track coach."

"At a Catholic high school?"

"No. For high school I switched to public school. They're at Madison."

The guard had been glowering at me for several minutes. I stood, and so did Jorge.

"I'll stay in touch," I said.

Jorge nodded.

As if leaving the table had been a signal, the door opened and Graciela rushed in. She was almost hobbling in the too-tight pumps. She exchanged a few quick words with her son in Spanish. Jorge said goodbye to me in English just before the guard hustled him out.

Graciela and I were escorted back to the gate, where the guard in the cage collected our badges and admitted us to the elevator.

"What do you think?" Graciela asked. "He's innocent, right?"

"I think he might be," I answered.

"Not might be. He is innocent. So what are you going to do now?"

"I'll talk to Miriam Stern tomorrow. I'll see what she's going to do."

"No. You leave it up to that girl, he'll never get out."

I stepped out of the elevator and walked ahead of Graciela to the parking lot. I had started the car and pulled out to the sidewalk by the time Graciela caught up. And I had turned up the radio to discourage conversation.

Graciela sat as tight-lipped on the way back as she had on the way there. She didn't speak until the car was in the garage and we were on the sidewalk.

"So what are you going to do now?" she repeated.

"The best I can," I said. "I'll let you know."

I walked up the front steps looking straight ahead. Graciela's eyes burned guilty holes in my back.

Amy and Mac were waiting on the porch.

"I don't know, guys," I told them. "There ought to be a less obtrusive place for you to hang out."

Mac lowered his head, certain he was being chastised for something. Amy stared at me, unblinking, equally certain that her own opinion was the only one that counted, whether she was being chastised or not.

I let them in, and was aware all over again, as if for the first time, of the hole in the cabinet where my stereo used to be. And I thought of the body in the street, wearing my stolen jacket. That was how this started. And now, here I was, trying to help the young man accused of murdering somebody who probably burgled my apartment. I shook my head and went on to the kitchen, where the cats were waiting to be fed.

Then I check the answering machine for the first time that day.

The message from Kirby was short: "Where the hell are you?"

I could ignore him for a while, but sooner or later I would have to return the call. First, though, I could call Dixie. Surely Dixie could see what was happening to Kirby, what had already happened to him. Surely Dixie would be grateful for my help.

And there was one more thing I could do before

calling Kirby. I could ask Carol about the two teachers at Madison High.

I went back down the stairs and across the street, relieved to postpone the moment of confrontation.

The woman who answered the door was a body-builder wearing jeans and a white tank top that emphasized her tanned biceps. She had curly blond hair sticking out from under a Dodgers cap, a broken nose, and the cool stare of someone who protected her territory.

"Hi," I said with as much cheer as I could muster. "Is Carol around?"

"Just a minute."

The woman walked away from the door without asking me in. I stayed on the porch.

Carol appeared a few seconds later.

"Hi," she said. "Come on in."

"It's okay. I don't want to disturb anyone."

Carol laughed. "Lisa gets a little testy. Come in if you want."

"I really just wanted to ask a couple of questions about Madison High. Jorge mentioned two teachers— Mr. Zaslov and Mr. Moreno—who might be willing to act as character witnesses. I'm going to give his lawyer a call in the morning, and I thought I'd offer as much information as I could."

"I know Ozzie Moreno slightly—he'll be out on the track field at least until five, so you can catch him anytime in the late afternoon, if you really want to. I don't think you'll get anything out of him, not even for Jorge. Bill Zaslov and I have different schedules, so I only know him by sight. But if you check with the office, you can find out when he has a free period."

I was going to explain that I didn't plan to go over there, but it didn't seem important. I just nodded.

"I gather you don't have any personal experience with Jorge at the high school," I said.

"Not a thing. I would have told you."

"Okay. Thanks."

"Sure you don't want to come in?"

"Not today, but thanks for asking. Say goodbye to Lisa for me."

I crossed the street and climbed the stairs to my home, hoping I was burning many calories in the process.

The phone call to Kirby loomed larger and larger as I climbed, and I decided to get it over with.

"You fiend! You blackguard!" he shouted in response to my hello.

I immediately regretted calling.

"You left again! You left me distraught, hysterical, mourning my best friend, all alone! Without even a word of goodbye! I turned my back for a moment, and you were gone. I am lost without you my baby darling, absolutely lost. When are you coming back?"

I wanted to shout "Never!" and hang up. Instead, I took a deep breath and answered him.

"You weren't alone. Gordo was there, and Gordo is your best friend. You were playing the piano, and you weren't hysterical. I suspect you didn't notice I'd left for hours."

"That begs the question. When are you coming back?"

"I don't know yet. I'll call you in a couple of days. We need to talk." That was the wrong thing to say, and I knew it as I said it.

"Talk? What is there to talk about? Why do women always want to talk? I've said what I have to say—I want you here, I want you with me."

"It isn't that simple, Kirby. Everything doesn't depend on what you want."

"If you're saying that being here isn't what you want, I can't believe you. I've known you too long. Being together is what you always wanted."

"Being together was what I wanted then. Things have changed. I've changed. Do you really want to have this discussion over the phone?"

He was silent for a moment. "All right, madame, we will talk in the flesh. When are you coming over?"

"I'll call in a day or two. Have you heard anything more about Tigger?"

"No. Although I doubt foul play."

"An overdose, Kirby. The police are going to tell you Tigger died of an overdose of cocaine or cocaine mixed with something. I think you know that."

He was silent again.

"You're right," he said finally. "I don't want to talk on the phone."

Our goodbyes were short and cool.

I put down the phone, regained my composure, and picked it up to call Dixie.

Dixie launched into an immediate gush about how glad she was to hear from me and what a wonderful time she had—we all had—the night before.

Dixie clearly hadn't heard about Tigger. And I didn't want to be the one to tell her. Cowardice kicked in again, the effect that the whole family had on me.

"I wondered if you were free for lunch one day this week," I said when Dixie paused for breath.

"That's a wonderful idea, Fay, and I would love to see you—we could have such fun together—but this week is terribly difficult. We start rehearsals for *Touch of the Poet* on Wednesday, and I have so much to do before then. Let's all have dinner again soon. I'll talk to Evan and call Kirby, and—''

''No, Dixie. I need to talk to you. It's about Kirby, and it's important. How about lunch tomorrow or Tuesday?''

''Tomorrow or Tuesday?'' Dixie's voice was an octave lower and ten degrees cooler. ''All right, dear, if it's that important. We can do lunch on Tuesday.''

Dixie and Evan lived in Laguna Niguel, in the same house they had bought twenty years before, when they decided not to do another series. Dixie agreed to meet me at a small cafe in Laguna Beach, noon on Tuesday.

I replaced the received and shut my eyes. I would have to rearrange my appointments at the clinic. This one time, I would have to let them down.

No. I would call Michael. He could cover for me. But I didn't have the energy for another phone call, not just then.

Sunday was over, and I hadn't even read the paper. I tried to laugh at myself for wanting to return to the routine trivia of my life. I hadn't thought about dinner, either.

I dragged my body to the kitchen and checked the refrigerator. There was stuff for a salad, there was broccoli and garlic and parmesan, and there was pasta in the cupboard. And there was milk and coffee for the morning.

I could do it. I could face it. I could prevail over all the death and disorder that was making me tired.

In the morning.

TEN

IN THE MORNING, I called Miriam Stern, who surprised me by being available.

"Great," Miriam responded after I brought her up to date. "You're doing a terrific job. I love it that the witness is a nice guy who might have doubts about what he saw. Do you think you could talk to those two teachers today?"

"What? I only agreed to cover the block. A task that would have been a lot easier if I had known Jorge saw a guy on a Harley, I might add. And I don't think there's any advantage in sending me to talk to Jorge's teachers."

"A big advantage. You're there. And I don't have time. I love it that his mother agreed that you're officially Jorge's therapist, too. You can spend a few hours with him before the trial, assessing his psychological state. You'll be a great witness. Better than the guy on the Harley. And if Jorge had told me about him, I would have told you, you know that. So you'll go?"

I started to protest, but I felt caught between Graciela Carrasco and Miriam Stern. Arguing with the two of them would take more time and energy than doing what they wanted.

"I'll talk to the teachers," I said. "I don't have a client until five. I'll let you know what they say."

"I'll be gone all afternoon. I'll call you tomorrow morning."

I hung up feeling put upon. But I looked up the number for Madison High and called it anyway. Bill Zaslov had a free period at two o'clock.

Having put it off until last, I called Michael and explained the situation.

"You want me to what?" he asked.

"Take my day at the clinic tomorrow," I repeated.

"I think my hearing is going."

"It won't be that bad. Really. Two appointments in the morning, two in the afternoon. And I'll make notes on each client—you can stop by tomorrow morning on your way in and pick them up. Please. Seeing Dixie is important to me."

"And your clients?" he asked.

"Of course they're important, too. But you're a good therapist, and it won't hurt you to be a practicing one for a day, and they might enjoy the change." I heard a pleading note creeping into my voice and stopped.

"I'll do it this time because I think you need to get past this Kirby McKenzie thing, and if that means lunch with his mother, then do it. But I don't want you to make a habit of this."

"Of course I won't make a habit of this." I said it as nicely as I could. This was not the moment to become annoyed. "And we'll have lunch Wednesday, on me. An early lunch," I added, remembering an afternoon appointment with a client.

"See you tomorrow morning."

One problem solved. Too many to go.

I left the house about twenty minutes before two, drove down Sunset to Griffith Park Boulevard, and then couldn't find a place to park. I wondered why the residents hadn't protested the clogging of the neighborhood, wondered even more how all those students found the money to buy cars.

The school probably pulled some wealthier students from the Los Feliz area, although I would have expected most of them to be in private schools. But this was pretty much a middle-class neighborhood, and twenty years or so earlier, when I was in high school, few middle-class students had cars. Now they had upgraded expectations that society wasn't prepared—or equipped—to meet.

Madison High was built from weathered bricks that would have had an early American patina except that every available inch of brick and concrete was covered with graffiti. Not simple black graffiti, the kind associated once with lavatory walls. This was graffiti in bold, primary colors, created with sweeping strokes of spray cans.

I decided to ask Richard about graffiti as art, the next time I saw him.

The front stairs led to a double glass door and a wide hall. The inside of the building, though cleaner, showed the telltale signs of cut budgets and deferred maintenance. A stopped clock hung on a wall that needed a coat of paint.

An open door beneath a sign that said Office was immediately to my left as I entered the building. A woman who appeared to be in her seventies was sitting behind the desk. Her gray hair was short and stylish and the lime green cotton blouse that hung from her bony shoulders was clean and neat. But her makeup was heavy and smeared, as if applied by a woman who needed glasses and wasn't wearing them, creating an effect something like a Picasso clown. A shaking hand tipped with Chinese red acrylic nails directed me down the hall toward Bill Zaslov's office, room 105.

There were two desks in room 105, and a man in his mid thirties wearing a blue work shirt and jeans was sitting at one of them, grading papers. Curly black hair with threads of gray brushed about his head. A mustache the same color bushed over his mouth. When I knocked on the edge of the open door, he looked up, and his jaw dropped.

"My God! Fay Cassidy!"

"What?" My jaw dropped in response.

"Fay Cassidy, what are you doing here? Come in, sit down."

I took the offered chair next to the desk, uncertain how to proceed.

"You don't remember me, do you?" The man was blushing.

"No, I'm sorry, but I don't." My heart was beating rapidly, and I was trying hard not to panic, hoping I hadn't met him when I was doing something truly embarrassing. Every once in a while a lost night from long ago shows up and smacks me in the face.

"It's all right. I'm Bill Zaslov. We only met a few times, at USC, and it has been a long time. I followed your career, thought, as long as you were on television."

I tried to imagine the face fifteen years younger and without the mustache, but he still didn't look familiar.

"Could you tell me how we met?" I asked.

"I knew Kirby McKenzie, from high school. Here. Madison High. We were buddies on the varsity football team."

"That makes it sound like a simpler time."

"Yes, I think it was. At USC, though, we went in separate directions. I majored in English, and as you know, Kirby headed for the theater department. We both knew there was no point in going out for football.

The Trojans are almost a farm team for the pros, and neither of us was that good.''

He was still blushing, still uncomfortable at having so obviously thrown my composure. I hoped I could think of something that would put him at ease, now that he had put me at mine.

''You still haven't told me how we met,'' I said.

''Backstage at *Two for the Seesaw*. I went to everything Kirby was in, and I always went backstage to say hello. After I met you, I came to things you were in and went backstage to say hello.''

''Of course. I remember now. Kirby introduced you as an old friend.'' That was a lie. But his face brightened, so it was a worthwhile one. And there was something vaguely familiar about him, now that we were talking.

''Do you ever see Kirby anymore?''

''I hadn't seen him for a long time. I've seen him recently, though.''

''Tell him hello, will you? Next time you see him? Tell him I'd like to hear from him, get together and talk about old times. He was such an amazingly talented human being—still is, I'm sure—I knew he'd be a star. I'm only surprised that he hasn't gone further, done even better, with his talent.''

''Yes, I know what you mean.'' I was becoming glad I had agreed to run the errand for Jorge. I had needed someone to remind me that I had been right about Kirby, right about the person he used to be. ''I'll tell him.''

''Thanks. And that isn't what you're here for.''

''No. I came to ask you about Jorge Carrasco.''

''I heard he's in trouble,'' Bill Zaslov said, frowning. ''And that's a surprise. Of all the kids around here,

I would have thought he was one of the least likely to end up in jail. What happened?''

"He's been charged with murder. And assault and battery on a police officer, and resisting arrest. It's a long story. The punchline is, his mother and his attorney talked me into helping.''

"Are you a social worker now? I've wondered what happened, why you stopped working as an actress.''

"I'm a therapist, and Jorge's neighbor. And I stopped working as an actress because nobody would hire me.''

"Sorry.'' He blushed again. "As for helping Jorge, you can add me to the list. None of that sounds like the kid I know.''

"Good. Jorge said you might be willing to come forward as a character witness.''

"Absolutely.'' Zaslov hesitated, then continued. "You said something about a simpler time. You're right. There was a mix of students when Kirby and I were here, but compared to what we have now, it was a homogeneous, middle-class bunch. Orderly and well-behaved. You could still get sent to the principal's office for saying hell or damn in class, can you believe that? Now we let the shits and fucks go right by, happy that they're swearing in English.''

I laughed, and he smiled in appreciation.

"Jorge's English is terrific,'' I said.

"You're right, it is. And learning English isn't the only problem for the kids. I have kids—seniors—in my class who can't read, write, or think in any language. And they've stayed in school. The dropout rate here is about thirty per cent, and not all of them from the bottom of the class, but a lot of them close to it. Then on top of the scholastic problems, we have to deal with the phenomenal explosion of violence. Some of it probably comes from the students' frustration at being caught in a system where they don't do well. Whatever the reasons for it, we're not coping well with the results. And I hadn't expected Jorge to fall victim.''

I hadn't expected the lecture. But he needed to talk, and I didn't want to cut him off.

"How bad is the violence?" I asked.

"We have security guards, all day, patrolling the building and the parking lots. Women teachers are encouraged to take self-defense classes, and never to stay too late in the afternoon. We are pretty much all agreed that a gun in the halls ought to be grounds for expulsion, but we argue about the knives. We might lose half of our male student body.'' He stopped and looked at me. ''You're probably wondering why I stay.''

"As a matter of fact, I am.''

"The simple answer is, somebody has to, and I'm already here. I don't believe we can afford to write off a whole generation of inner city kids, and we're awfully close to doing just that. The more complex answer has to do with the good students—and there are some good students here. The top students here can compete with the top students anywhere, and have.''

"Wait—I remember you, not from USC, but more recently. You were the coach of the Madison High team that beat Beverly Hills High in the Scholastic Olympics.''

Bill Zaslov finally relaxed.

"Two years in a row,'' he said proudly. ''We beat them two years in a row. That's what I mean about the good students. They can do it, and I'm not willing to give up on them. At the same time, I'm not sure how much longer I can stay. Burnout is on the horizon.''

"Jorge wasn't on the team, was he?''

"No. But that doesn't mean he isn't good. We really do have more than five good students, although I don't know that I could get much past fifty."

"How well do you know Jorge? Would you have known if he joined a gang?"

"Probably. That's usually something students broadcast. They wear the colors and hang out with other gang members. Jorge never did. And I would have noticed. This is the second year he's been in one of my classes."

"An English class?"

"Yes, but this is an honors class, for students who don't need the grammar drills. Essentially, it's a creative writing class, although I make them read a lot, too. It's a small class, a lot of work, and they have to test to get into it. I encouraged Jorge to enroll on the basis of the work he did last year. And I haven't been disappointed." Zaslov paused and looked at the papers on his desk. "I'll find something of his to show you another time. He isn't a budding Garcia Marquez or anything, but he has a sense of style, and his humor comes through. He has a lot of promise, and there isn't enough of it around. I don't want to see it wasted."

"That was more or less my reaction."

"Do you know how he's doing in jail?"

"I saw him yesterday—I'm officially his therapist. He's holding up. He doesn't seem bitter, and I think I would be."

"I think I would be, too." Zaslov glanced at his watch, then again at the papers on his desk. "I hate cutting this off, but I've got to get some work done before three. Could we continue another time?"

"Sure. Could you point me toward the track field?"

"Ozzie Moreno?"

I nodded.

"There's your bitter Hispanic," Zaslov said. "Although I shouldn't complain about him. The kids like him, and the sports program is one of the few unifying forces here. Down the hall, out the door, through the parking lot, past the baseball diamond. And good luck with Ozzie."

"Thanks."

I followed his directions.

The parking lot was jammed with ten-year-old cars so close together that the asphalt must have been littered with paint chips at the end of each day. An occasional gem not more than five years old had towels hanging outside its windows, in a stab at protecting the finish. The stickers in the windows proclaimed this the faculty-staff lot.

I skirted the baseball diamond, where a tall, rangy black man was batting fungo to a rag-tag collection of fielders, and took a careful seat in the front row of the scarred bleachers beside the track oval. I had made what now seemed to be the mistake of wearing a skirt rather than jeans, because I had wanted to look professional, and I didn't want snags in the fabric or splinters in the flesh.

And I was wearing silver jewelry, of course. One indication of how the stress was piling up, how consuming my involvement in this situation had become, was that I hadn't dashed out to replace my gold jewelry and my stereo.

But a trip to the downtown jewelry mart was in order, and surely Michael would go along, before our Wednesday lunch. I perked up at the thought of listening to him talk about Elizabeth, as a break from the problems everyone else was presenting me with.

I had been idly watching about a dozen young men in tank tops and shorts jogging around the track, wondering where Ozzie Moreno was, when I realized that one of the young men wasn't quite as boyish as the others. The thing that happens to the outlines of bodies as people age—not weight or fitness, but veins, or skin tone, or something—had happened to the body in front, the one pacing the others. That one belonged to an adult.

I watched for several laps, until the man called out something in Spanish that I couldn't understand but the boys obviously could. They all trotted toward the same part of the field and lined up.

The man trotted more slowly over to the bleachers, not far from me, and picked up a towel.

"Mr. Moreno?" I asked, disengaging my skirt from the bench and walking toward him.

"Yeah. What?" He was sweating, but he wasn't short of breath.

"I'm Faith Cassidy. I wanted to talk to you for a minute. Jorge Carrasco is in jail—you probably know that—and he said you might be willing to testify as a character witness."

Moreno had wiped the sweat from his face and neck and was working on his arms.

"Jorge is a good kid, and a good distance runner. But if he is caught in the Anglo court system, there is nothing I can do. And nothing you can do, either. Why does your husband allow you to go on fool's errands like this?"

"Well—I don't have a husband, and I don't need permission—" I had taken offense, and I realized immediately that I had made a mistake. I could tell that from his eyes. But there was no good way out of it.

"You don't have a husband? Maybe I see you later then."

"I don't think so."

"Why not, puta?"

I froze. My Spanish was limited, but I knew that word.

Moreno looked at me, pleased at the impact.

"I'm sorry I bothered you," I said. "And I'm even sorrier that Jorge respects you."

I turned and stalked away, not looking back. I forced my shaking muscles to keep going until I reached my car. Then I opened the door and sat on the edge of the seat, legs outside, so that I could put my head between my knees.

There was no reason for me to faint or vomit just because some asshole caught me offguard and called me a whore when I was doing a favor for somebody. It's just that I had expected a round of applause. And Moreno had booed me. And I hadn't realized until the disapproval hit my gut how much I had actually been enjoying the role of detective.

When my vital signs were back to normal, I drove home.

Norman was standing on his porch, shouting.

I hurried out of the car, then slowly got back in and drove it into the garage when I heard the word "music."

Norman had retreated to the house by the time I started up the steps.

"Hey, girl, stop over for a minute."

The call came from the other direction.

Marcus's naked chest was curled around his kitchen door.

I stepped across the low fence separating the two yards, through the squashed place in the ivy that Louie and I had created going back and forth.

Louie and I had a deal, that he could come over for coffee any time he wanted if I could throw him out any time I wanted. I considered telling Louie about Richard's coffee. And realized that I was thinking about Richard again.

Marcus had disappeared by the time I reached his door.

"Hello," I called, walking in.

Marcus padded back into the kitchen, a short red and black robe hanging over his jockey shorts.

"Gimme a kiss," he ordered holding out his cheek.

I pecked the air next to his skin.

"What's wrong with Norman?" I asked.

"Is something wrong? I been playing a little music here, all by myself, and I guess I just tuned out the background noise."

Marcus grinned, and I laughed.

"What did you call me over for—other than to make him angrier?"

"I don't need a reason to talk to you, now, do I?"

"No, but I suspect you have one."

"Well, I just thought you might want to know, I saw that redheaded dude, the one Louie saw right before your house was hit. He was hanging out at the corner last night."

"Are you certain it was the same man?"

"Not for sure. But you don't see too many redheads in this neighborhood, especially in the middle of the night."

"What was he doing?"

"Just hanging out at the corner, like he was waiting for something. Or someone."

"You think maybe it was a drug buy?"

"Could be." Marcus nodded solemnly. "Could be something else, who knows?"

"Marcus, why are you telling me today? Why the hell didn't you call the cops last night?"

"It was late, and I was tired, and I figured the guy would be gone by the time the cops got here anyway."

"Great." I tried to get angry, but Marcus smiled at me. I shook my head. "I don't know what I can do with the information, but thanks for telling me anyway. And speaking of information I don't need, I found the witness who called the police. A neighbor. Not a party guest."

"That's a relief. I figured any guest who saw something would have talked to me before the police. Good to know my trust was not misplaced."

"Ladies and gentlemen, one and all." I kissed him on the cheek—a generous smack—and said goodbye.

I picked my way across the low fence, glad Norman had stopped yelling.

Amy and Mac were waiting on the porch.

"If you're going to do this," I said to Amy, "you might learn to attack. Or at least dial 911."

Amy stared as if she understood but didn't care. Mac scrunched down next to his mother, but only until the door was open. They both trotted in behind me, then went straight on to the kitchen.

"I've only been gone a little while," I yelled. "You have food."

There was a message from Carol on the answering machine, saying that Eunice Hsieh had agreed to ask her parents if they had seen anything, but warning me not to count on it.

I punched out Michael's number and got his machine.

"Lunch Wednesday is now downtown," I said. "I've decided a visit to the jewelry mart is in order. And I have to tell you about the Jorge Carrasco situation. It seems I'm still on the case."

ELEVEN

MIRIAM STERN WOKE ME UP the next morning, apologizing for the hour, and explaining that she had to be in court.

"Bill Zaslov will be an asset," I told her, "but Ozzie Moreno won't. And it seems to me that we ought to be approaching this from another perspective, too. My next-door neighbors have seen a man twice now, late at night, who doesn't live on this block. So something else may be going on. What if the murder was—just for example—a drug deal gone wrong?"

"We can't suggest that in court without evidence. You may remember a famous case in which someone tried." She said it with dry humor. The O.J. Simpson murder trial didn't have to be cited by name. "And collecting evidence would be both difficult and dangerous, if it really was a drug deal gone wrong."

"What do you think I should do?"

"Nothing dangerous. Nothing you weren't planning to do anyway. Stay alert, ask your neighbors to stay alert, and if you come up with anything, let me know."

"It may be time for another meeting of the Watch. Is there anything new on the identity of the murdered man? That would be an excuse to get people together."

"I'll let you know. For now, he's Adam 103. And the police aren't expecting anyone to claim him."

After I hung up, I decided that being up early and alert was a good idea. Michael would be over soon to get notes on my clients, and then I was meeting Dixie in Laguna Beach.

Michael barely said hello and goodbye.

"We'll save it all for lunch tomorrow," he said.

Dressing for lunch with Dixie was easier than dressing for dinner had been, but I was still intimidated, and still without gold jewelry. I settled on pale green linen jacket and pants and was grateful that I still had silver.

May is probably beautiful everywhere in the Northern Hemisphere, and everyone says the weather in L.A. is always great, even though it isn't true. But there is something special about May in Southern California. By the time I had driven half an hour south of the city that day, once I had passed Knott's Berry Farm, Disneyland, and the congestion of Santa Ana, I found a countryside still green from the winter rains and a sky shockingly clear and blue, not yet subject to the dreary cloud cover of June that segues through heat and humidity into the smog of August.

The civilization creep is worse every year, and I don't doubt that one of these days there will be houses from Santa Barbara to San Diego. In the meantime, I could enjoy the strawberry fields, and the hills dotted with scrub oak and sumac.

I took the Laguna Freeway to the winding canyon road, followed it until the pine trees gave way to cottage businesses, mostly arts related.

Laguna Beach was a former artists' colony turned tourist center, much like Carmel or Aspen, but still undeniably charming. I parked in a public lot about three blocks from the beach and strolled past pseudo-rustic art galleries and gift shops, built from distressed wood and shiny plate glass.

The cafe was little more than hanging plants and open air. Dixie was waiting at one of the sidewalk tables.

"You look so beautiful, Fay dear," Dixie said, kissing the air next to my cheek and then settling back in her chair before I had a chance to respond in kind. "I can't believe it's been fifteen years since you and Kirby broke up."

"I can't either, Dixie. You haven't changed at all."

That was almost true. Dixie had to be in her sixties, but she had an ageless radiance that other women spent futile dollars on surgery and cosmetics trying to achieve. It was partly the cheekbones, I thought, then remembered that Kirby had said that about me. Dixie hadn't gained weight, though, so that all the years had done, all the graying of her hair had done, was to soften the lines of her face. Her skin, without makeup, was lightly tanned, a deep, shining gold next to her white cotton tunic.

I had felt out-glamoured on Saturday night, and this day I felt out-simplified. I wasn't certain why my relationship with Dixie always felt like a competition that I was doomed to lose.

"Haven't changed? There was a time when I would have played the daughter in *Touch of the Poet,* not the mother. I know I've changed. The only consolation is that the mother is a better role. There aren't many parts for old women on television, but some great ones have been written for the theater. And the theater is more fun. Less money, more work, but more fun."

Dixie was smiling as she hit the word "work," and

I got the subtext. Dixie was telling me that she wasn't going to waste a lot of time on lunch.

A young, blond waiter arrived almost immediately and bowed to Dixie. I hadn't thought surfers bowed, but Dixie could inspire respect from a turnip. He placed a basket of warm rolls and a small cup of whipped butter between us.

Dixie ordered a small seafood salad and mineral water. I took the same.

"I can't tell you how happy I was when Kirby said that you were coming Saturday night," Dixie said once the waiter had bowed his way to the kitchen. "I have prayed so often that you two would get back together. You were the only woman Kirby has ever cared about who had a head on her shoulders. Not that I didn't like Tara, but that poor girl always behaved as if her mind were off in space somewhere, and that was a shame, because I really thought she had a career ahead of her when I first met her."

"Maybe she did," I said, breaking one of the crusty rolls. "I don't know the story—except Kirby's remark that Tara was gone with the wind—but I can guess at least part of it."

"What do you mean?"

"Did Tara by any chance spend some time in a hospital, a place like Betty Ford's, for example, right before she asked for a divorce?"

"I have no idea. I know there was some kind of trial separation before the divorce, but I didn't ask where Tara was spending it."

"Oh, great, Dixie, just great." That came out harder than I had intended.

"I don't interfere in my son's life, Fay. You must be aware of that. That was the deal, if you remember, when he agreed to stay in college until graduation. I would never interfere again. And I have lived up to it. I was willing to meet you today to discuss Kirby only because I have loved you so much over the years, and I know you have Kirby's best interests at heart.'' Dixie's cold eyes took the life out of her words.

"Are you aware that Kirby has a drug problem?"

"Absolutely not." She didn't even blink. "I know he drinks—problems with booze run in the family, and a lot of actors have that trouble. But not drugs."

"Yes. Drugs." I hadn't planned to open the subject before the food arrived. I wished I had been able to make small talk with Dixie first. Since I had leapt into it, though, I would proceed. I looked at Dixie without flinching. "Cocaine, to be precise. I know Kirby has always been a heavy drinker. He probably drank too much even when we were in college, but in those days it just made him seem like one of the boys. This is different. Kirby has a heavy cocaine habit. And the booze makes it worse."

"I don't believe it. Kirby is too smart and too talented to get into anything he can't control."

I opened my mouth to reply and closed it again when the smiling waiter appeared with salads and mineral water.

"Is there anything else, Mrs. McKenzie?" he asked.

"Not now, dear."

The waiter looked as if he might genuflect and kiss her ring. "Just wave if you need me."

I let him take two steps backward before starting in again.

"I would have agreed with you about Kirby fifteen years ago. I want to agree with you now. But I can't."

"Why are you saying this?"

"I've seen him. I didn't want to see what was happening, and I certainly didn't want to be part of it, but I'm not blinded by love any longer."

"Let me sort this out." Dixie's long, thin fingers were clasped lightly above her salad plate. "Are you part of what you say is going on? Do you use cocaine?"

"I did use cocaine. At one time, I used too much. I don't now. I slipped last Wednesday with Kirby, for the first time in years. I know what I'm talking about." This wasn't going the way I had anticipated. I hadn't intended to say that.

"I see. I think there's a word in your new profession for what's going on here. Projection? Isn't that it? You had a cocaine problem that ruined your career. Therefore Kirby has a cocaine problem that is ruining his."

"I haven't asked about his career problems," I said. "I'm only concerned with his drug problem."

"And I'm supposed to take your word for it, after you've admitted a problem of your own. If you wanted to tell me that you and Kirby are not getting back together, and wanted to blame that on Kirby, you could have done that over the phone. This charade isn't necessary."

"Goddamn it, Dixie. The word in my new profession for what's going on is denial." I snapped it at her, then did my best to soften my tone. "Yes, I'm telling you we aren't getting back together. And I'm telling you why. But this isn't about blame, it's about help. I want you to work with me to help Kirby."

"Kirby can help himself."

"Did he tell you that we found Tigger, his drummer, dead on the doorstep Saturday night? Did he tell you that?"

Dixie hesitated no more than a second. "No, he didn't. He told me that Tigger died, but he spared me details that were obviously causing him a great deal of pain. And I don't know how you think you can link Tigger's death to Kirby, other than that the poor young man chose Kirby's home to come to when he knew he was in trouble. Whether drugs were involved in Tigger's death is beside the point. Kirby has always opened his home to those in need, as a sanctuary. I shouldn't have to tell you that."

I wanted to respond, but Dixie barely paused for breath.

"I haven't always approved of the friends I found there," she continued, "and I was frankly hoping that was something you could change. But to say that he encourages, or even sanctions, the use of cocaine, or that he has used it himself, beyond some boyish experiment, is an accusation I will not tolerate."

"I can't help what you will or will not tolerate. I can only tell you what's happening. The situation—his cocaine use—is beyond his control. He's in trouble, and if I stayed, it wouldn't help him, it would only hurt me. Unless you want to help, too."

I stared at Dixie, and Dixie stared back, both with our eyes wide, mouths set, fists clenched on the table top. This time, Dixie flinched.

"I'm sorry, Fay. I hadn't realized how short my time was going to be this afternoon. I'm afraid I'm going to have to run."

Before I could recover, Dixie pulled two twenties from her wallet and dropped them on the table.

"Take your time, dear, and enjoy your lunch."

I shut my eyes, unable to watch Dixie leave.

"Is something wrong?"

I opened them again to behold the worried face of the young blond waiter.

"Mrs. McKenzie didn't touch her salad," he added.

"No. Nothing's wrong. She just lost track of the time. And don't take the salad away. I'm hungrier than I thought."

The sun was shining, the tourists were gawking, the sea was rippling with little waves so small and cheerful that the surfers could only mope about on the sand, and I was not going to deal with other people's problems anymore, not until I had eaten. The dubious expression on the waiter's face bothered me not at all.

"And I'd like a double latte in about twenty minutes," I told him. "When I'm finished with the salads."

By the time I left the restaurant, I was pleasantly full. And certain I deserved the free lunch.

The drive back to the city was never quite as much fun as the drive away. There was always that moment when the skyscrapers rose out of a faint haze and I realized that even a clear day in Los Angeles isn't what the rest of the world means by clear.

I used the drive to sort through my feelings about Kirby and Dixie, and as I signaled to change lanes for the exit ramp, I was down to relief that at least I had done my best, and my confrontation with Dixie was over.

I had turned the corner onto my own block when the Harley roared up next to me.

Richard looked so much the stereotypical biker in jeans, T-shirt, denim vest, headband, and dark goggles and helmet that he would have made me nervous if I hadn't already met him. He motioned toward his apart-

ment building. I pointed to my garage. He nodded and
followed.

"I'll give you a ride," he said once the car was
inside. "Hop on."

Hopping was not the right word for what I did. I
managed to throw one leg across the bike behind him
and struggle onto the seat. I held on to the edges of his
vest as he made a u-turn and gunned down the block,
through the open gate, and down the driveway into his
parking space.

"That was fun," I said, flustered.

I dismounted as awkwardly as I had gotten on. While
he was locking the bike, I dug my brush out of my
purse and tried to coax the wind-whipped strands back
into shape.

"I'm glad you like it," he said. He opened one of
his saddlebags and retrieved a plastic sack of groceries.
"Come on up—I'll fix you a cup of coffee."

"Done."

Another cup of coffee would keep me wired for the
evening and maybe into the night, but I didn't want to
turn down the invitation. I followed him up the stairs
and into the apartment.

In just two days, the painting had taken form. Hills,
sky, and houses all showed traces of color. A collection
of paint tubes and what looked like a tool kit of brushes
and other supplies were littered on the newspapers beneath the easel. He had been working since I had seen
him. A lot.

"This is amazing," I said, when Richard returned
from the kitchen and handed me a mug almost overflowing with steamed milk. "You've done so much."

"That's because I do it all in my head before I

start,'' he said. ''I may think for months, and then paint it in a week.''

He made a gesture toward the canvas, full of raw energy and grace, that reminded me of Cyrano with a sword.

''Sit,'' he said, ''and tell me how your quest for justice is coming.''

''I'm glad you asked.'' This time I settled onto a purple-and-green striped cotton pillow. ''Have you seen a strange redhead in the middle of the night?''

''How do I answer that? Only in my nightmares? Not since my ex-wife moved to Texas? Tell me more.'' He sat on the orchid pillow, across the room.

''My next-door neighbors have seen a redheaded man who doesn't live around here twice, late at night. And I'm wondering if there is drug dealing going on.''

''And if there is?''

''Then the attorney can come up with some scenarios for the kid's murder in the street more likely than Jorge Carrasco's initiation into a gang. Particularly since the kid was probably the perp who burglarized my house, which the police thought at the time was for drug money.''

''Are these scenarios that the police will buy?''

''Not yet. And that's where you can help.'' I ignored his dubious look. I wasn't through improvising. The painting captured the view to the northwest. But he had another window, one facing due north. I pointed to it. ''You can see the entire block from that window. You could stake out the street for a night or two, watch for drug activity.''

''I can? Who volunteered me?''

''I did,'' I said firmly. ''You meet all the tests. You are a principled human being who wouldn't want to see a miscarriage of justice, and you have the window with a view. Nobody else involved can see the whole block.''

''Okay. I'll do it. But you have to sit up and watch with me.'' He was smiling as he said it, blue eyes crinkling.

''You're on.''

''What night do we pick? Or do we figure that drug buys happen every night of the week?''

I knew he wasn't taking this seriously, and I was a little annoyed.

''They probably do, but I suggest we try Friday, since the murder happened on a Friday night. How does Friday work for you?''

''Fine. Friday's fine.''

''Good. Since you're providing the window, I'll bring dinner. Nine o'clock?''

''See you then.''

I finished my coffee, said goodbye, and walked the short block home. Amy and Mac were sitting on the porch, and Amy was glaring. She had seen me ride away on the Harley.

''Come on,'' I said. I picked up Mac and hugged him.

The casual physical contact on the Harley had felt good. Drug buy or not, I was looking forward, with only a tiny bit of trepidation, to Friday evening.

TWELVE

"SO MANY CHOICES!" I wailed, looking at the vast room full of jewelry showcases.

The jewelry mart was just north of the garment district, in downtown Los Angeles. There were actually several locations to choose from, each one stretching for most of a block, eclectic collections of independent jewelers, mostly importers from Asia or the Mideast, displaying their shining, twinkling, gleaming, and truly enticing wares.

I had dragged Michael to what seemed to be the largest of the bazaars, walking uncomfortably past the ragged, vacant-eyed castoffs of an affluent society that clogged the midcity sidewalks and huddled in boarded-up doorways. Inside, value-conscious secretaries sifted through strings of freshwater pearls, stockbrokers weighed solid gold cufflinks in their white hands, and security guards made certain that no one was disrupted.

"Have you decided what you're looking for?" Michael asked.

"Gold earrings and a gold chain, I told you."

We were walking slowly down an aisle, watches and cufflinks on one side, chains and earrings on the other.

"Not specific enough. The more specific your goals are, the easier they are to achieve."

"Oh, bah. Tell that to your clients. I'll know what I

want when I see it." I stopped and pointed to a pair of gold hoop earrings wrapped with a filigreed wire. "How much?"

The man behind the counter, whose Mediterranean brown skin made his open-necked white shirt glow, weighed the earrings, multiplied the weight times something on a calculator, and told me the amount. We went through the same ritual with a gold chain.

I gave him a credit card.

"Next time you come in I will sell you a wedding ring," he said, smiling as he handed me the package.

Michael had moved on to another case, and I didn't bother explaining to the clerk the error of his assumptions.

"I wonder how much that gold rope around his neck is worth," I asked when I caught up with Michael.

"If you have to ask," Michael began.

"I can't afford it," I finished. "Are you buying something?"

"I haven't decided. Do you think I should get an ear pierced?"

"If you're going to get anything pierced, I think it ought to be an ear. I had both of mine pierced twenty years ago, before it occurred to me to be appalled that I could engage in the barbaric practice of mutilating my flesh for the sake of adornment. They got infected, and they hurt for weeks. I'm glad it's done, but I wouldn't do it again."

"I'll think about it a while longer. Are you through shopping?"

"For the moment. I'm ready for lunch."

We left the mart and turned right on Hill, walking toward the financial district, and stopped at the first air-conditioned coffee shop in a high-rise bank building that we found.

I had thought about suggesting that we walk east instead, toward an area with a couple of restaurants that catered to the loft crowd, but decided I didn't want to risk running into Richard right then. I would have to introduce him to Michael and explain them to each other.

A waitress showed us to a clean, white plastic table and handed us menus.

I pulled out my glasses to take a look. I wished I had pushed for a place with a more interesting selection, then settled on the tomato-avocado-cheese club sandwich. Michael ordered the chicken salad.

"For the second time today, how did it go with Dixie?" he asked. He had asked the first time on the way downtown, but I had put him off, wanting to hear about his day with my clients instead.

Only one had cancelled when she realized a man was filling in, and two had actually enjoyed the encounter. I was glad it went well and sorry I wasn't missed a little more.

But I had to tell him about Dixie.

"I hate to say that you were right, but you were. She refused to admit that he has a problem."

"So you're going to drop the whole idea of a Kirby intervention and walk away? Good!"

I shook my head. "It's not that simple. I remember who he was, and who I thought he was going to be, and I'm not certain I can walk away that easily."

"Whoever he used to be, Faith, he's a drug-addicted asshole now. And you must see that."

"I do. I still see the memories, though. He used to be so funny, doing his Toshiro Mifune imitation in the bathtub. And romantic. He'd dash out to cut roses for me at two in the morning. When I was in a disastrous production of *The Trojan Women*—truly disastrous, so disastrous that two hundred people left at intermission on opening night—''

''Two hundred people? What were two hundred people doing at a university production of *The Trojan Women?*''

''The season was heavily subscribed by alumni, and four hundred people were there for the opening, a full house, and half of them left at the break. I was hysterical the next day, and I didn't want to go back that night, I wanted to call in sick, tell them my mother had died, anything.''

''It couldn't have been your fault that the show was awful,'' Michael said sympathetically.

''It wasn't. I was only in the chorus. And everyone knows *The Trojan Women* should be performed without an intermission. Anyway, I had to go to do the show, and I was all set to leave, when Kirby grabbed me and kissed me and started to undress me. We made love on the floor, and then I had to hurry, and I was getting dressed, and he stopped me and said, 'Now— you are going to have a good time tonight. You are going to have a good time driving to the university, a good time finding a place to park, a good time putting your makeup on, and a good time doing the show.' And I did.''

''You did what Kirby told you to do.''

It seemed like a good idea at the time,'' I said, annoyed that Michael couldn't understand the pull of memories, the old attraction revisited. ''I'm not sure I could have done it just because Kirby told me to. But as I got into the car, I realized my sweater was on inside out, and I didn't have time to do anything about it. And I started to laugh. I laughed all the way to the school, all the way to the dressing room, and when the other actresses threatened to bar me from the mirror until I stopped laughing, I started singing, *Put on a Happy Face*. The absurdity of it got to everyone. They all started laughing and singing.''

"And the show was a hit after all, thanks to Kirby?"

"I wish it had been. It wasn't. It was still the worst production I ever had to survive twelve performances of, but I couldn't have done it without Kirby."

"I don't believe that. I believe you would have been just fine without him then, and you're better off without him now."

The waitress arrived with my sandwich and Michael's salad.

"Maybe." I wanted the sandwich, but I had to finish the part about Kirby first. "And speaking of my mother dying, he was there for that, too, and he was important to my surviving again. And that's only part of why I flirted with the idea of going back."

"I won't try to argue with your feelings, Faith. But I hope the flirtation is only an idle one."

"It's all right, Michael. I promise. And I may be flirting with someone else." That came out before I really thought about it. "I'm having dinner Friday night with the so-called witness to the crime. He's an artist, and he's sort of attractive."

"'Sort of attractive' is the highest compliment you've paid a man in three years."

"I know, and that scares me. I'm having dinner with him anyway, though. We're going to watch the street. In fact, I'm fixing dinner."

Michael blinked. "You're fixing dinner? You haven't fixed more than a salad or an omelet for yourself as long as I've known you. And you don't entertain. That sounds even more promising than 'sort of attractive.'"

"I make sandwiches and I do all kinds of pasta, as

long as it doesn't have to bake. I can come up with something. I thought you'd pick up on 'watch the street.'''

"Oh. All right. Why are you going to be watching the street with this sort of attractive man you're fixing dinner for?"

I glared. "The body—which Miriam Stern informs me is now Adam 103—was wearing my jacket, and while there were no fingerprints to tie him to my burglary, I'm willing to make the leap. Absolutely everyone thought it was a drug money burglary. But no drugs were found on Adam 103. Thus, he bought, or attempted to buy, some chemical happiness, and something went wrong. No money and no drugs on the body when the police found it. I was there, remember? I really think we could at least inject reasonable doubt into the case against Jorge."

"Now he's Jorge?"

"Since I talked to him in the jail. His mother made me do it, but I'm not sorry. I'm officially his therapist, so I can visit any time I want."

"Are you telling me that you're going to be spending the evening with a sort of attractive man watching the street for drug deals? Please say you're not telling me that."

"Okay." I picked up my sandwich. Michael had been eating while I talked, and I was hungry.

"Faith, that's dangerous. I can't believe the attorney wants you to watch for a drug deal. Isn't there another way the police can find the murderer?"

"It's not dangerous to watch. Besides, as long as the police have Jorge, they're not likely to look for someone else. And without an identity for Adam 103, they wouldn't have many places to look." I put my sandwich back down. "I don't think the DA will drop the case against Jorge, and Miriam Stern doesn't want to plea bargain because she believes he's innocent. That means he goes to trial. And Miriam Stern can't introduce an alternate theory of the crime without some evidence. I would love to trust the system, believe that a jury of Jorge's peers would acquit him, but I think we need more than his word that he didn't do it. And the jury is unlikely to be made up of his peers. Evidence that someone is making drug deals on the street where Adam 103 was found can only help."

"Will you proceed cautiously?"

"I will. Now you talk about something so that I can finish my sandwich. Are you seeing the waiter?"

"If you're talking about the actor who served us brunch three days ago, I am not seeing him. I eat lunch at that cafe frequently—although I do cook for myself, as you know. When afternoons are slow, he sometimes joins me for a second latte. That's all."

"But you're thinking about it."

"Thinking slowly and cautiously. I'll let you know if there's more." Michael held up his water glass. "To caution."

"Right." I clicked with my iced tea glass and drank.

We finished lunch quickly because I didn't want to find another client waiting on the steps. And I insisted on picking up the check.

Michael dropped me off at home in plenty of time to pick up and return telephone messages before the scheduled appointment.

But the only message on the machine was from Kirby. I wondered if Dixie had told him about our meeting. It shouldn't matter—nothing could make things worse—but I didn't want Kirby yelling at me.

I also didn't want him calling me repeatedly with a client coming.

I picked up the phone and called him.

"I thought you might want to know, madame, that it was just as you suspected. My friend Andrew Smith, aka Tigger, died of heart failure brought on by the amount of cocaine in his bloodstream," Kirby said.

"Do you think he did it on purpose?"

"No, madame, I do not, and neither do the authorities." There was a long pause before he added, "They think he didn't realize how pure it was. Most of the blow around here has been cut, how much depending on how many hands it's been through. This was almost straight from the Colombian refinery."

"You knew, didn't you?"

"I beg your pardon?"

"That's what you meant when you said, 'What am I going to do?' You had scored the stuff, and you gave it to Tigger without warning him."

"Will you derive some perverse satisfaction from adding guilt to my grief?"

"No. No, I won't. What I said was lousy, and I'm sorry. I'm even sorrier if it's true."

There was another long pause.

"I had hoped I might persuade you to have dinner with me tonight," he finally said.

"No. I'm sorry, but no. This just isn't a good idea."

"Goodbye, madame."

The phone clicked in my ear.

Kirby had said the words with such finality that I considered rushing over to his house, in case he might be suicidal.

Kirby was dramatic, I decided, not suicidal. He would enjoy it if I rushed over, but I would not.

I would probably have to see him again, but only if I believed I could help. At that moment, I didn't.

My one appointment of the afternoon was uneventful. And by evening I was thinking again about Michael's comment, that I never cooked. It was more or less true, and I had actually intended to order Friday's dinner from one of the local restaurants that specialized in take-out.

But there was no reason why I couldn't make a picnic.

The next day I would be at the clinic, and I had three clients on Friday—including Jack Griffin—which meant I had to plan it right then.

"How long has it been since we've checked a cook book?" I asked Amy.

Amy looked back at me solemnly.

"I don't eat meat, and I don't know how he feels about fish, so it hasta be pasta," I said.

Amy didn't blink.

I found a recipe for a pasta salad with broccoli and red pepper that I thought would work. I could fix artichokes for appetizers. The grocery next to the clinic had some beautiful ones—and they had fruit, too. A loaf of good bread and a bottle of wine would fill out the menu.

Thinking about it made me so hungry that I stuck a package of frozen lasagna in the microwave and then ate it all.

I made it an early evening so that I could be up early in the morning. I had to prepare to face the clinic.

Walking in was even more embarrassing than I had expected, since not only Mary but all of my clients felt it necessary to bring up my illness of the week before. I bit my tongue and swallowed my shame and didn't tell them that I had only been hungover.

Mary had been doubly concerned when Michael had

filled in on Tuesday, even though he had assured her that I was all right.

"I'm all right," I told her again.

She looked at me as if it would be awhile before she trusted me.

"Elena is waiting," she said.

I got to work.

And I got everything for Friday's dinner except the bread and the wine from the small grocery store when I left the clinic for the day.

On Friday morning I drove to an upscale market in the Los Feliz area to find fresh baked bread and Chardonnay. I left and returned before noon, to make certain I was on time for Jack Griffin's appointment.

For the first time, he was late.

"I hope you didn't mind waiting," he said.

"Not as long as you had a reason to be late," I answered. "Sit down and tell me about it."

"I got tied up with a client," he said, a slight edge to his voice. "When I got into real estate, all you had to do was show up, you know? Houses sold themselves. Now you have to practically fucking beg to close a fucking deal."

"That must be very stressful for you."

"Goddamn right it's stressful. And do you think Linda understands that?"

"I don't know. What do you think?"

"I think she got stuck in a time warp, in the eighties, when greed was good. That's what I think."

"Have you asked her to listen to you?"

"Not after the first time, when I had to promise to listen to her. Since then, I haven't asked."

"That doesn't sound as if things are going well between you." I had to work to keep from taking Linda's side. "At some point, you'll have to talk to each other and listen to each other."

"Or end it."

"Is that what you're thinking of doing?"

"Yeah. But I haven't figured out how to do it without getting caught."

"You mean financially?"

"No, for Christ's sake. I mean by the police. The husband is the first one they check when a wife is offed."

I gripped the arms of my chair in what I hoped was an unobtrusive manner.

"Jack, if you have fantasies about violence, we can talk about them. I have to warn you, though, that if I believe that you might seriously harm your wife, I am required by law to take action."

"No. You're not going to do that. You care too much to do that. I know you."

"I do care. And if I thought you were planning to hurt Linda, caring would mean stopping you."

"Okay, kid, I hear you." Jack held out his hands in a gesture of surrender. "Let me tell you about my mother. I want you to understand why I get so upset about people being late."

I listened with part of my mind to a long story about entering kindergarten, when Jack thought his mother would be there at noon to pick him up, and she didn't come back until three.

The rest of my mind was wondering how I could refer him to someone else. His problems were more serious than any I was equipped to deal with.

I counted the minutes until the time was up.

"What do you mean?" Jack countered, bristling. "I got ten more minutes."

"You were ten minutes late," I said. "That doesn't mean you get ten minutes added at the end."

"I got ten minutes added when you were late."

"That's true. I took responsibility."

"So take it now."

"Fine. Talk." This didn't seem like the moment to argue.

Jack had hunched forward in the chair, ready to take me on. He wasn't ready to settle back and talk for ten minutes.

"That's okay," he said, standing. "I'll take responsibility. I'll see you next week. Hey, maybe it's time to make this twice a week. What do you think?"

"Why do you want to do that?"

"We could talk more. I could tell you how my mother died."

That caught me. "When do you want to come in?"

"Tomorrow?"

"Not Saturday. How about Wednesday at two?"

"Best you can do?"

"Yes." That was a lie. I was grateful for all those months on *Coffee Break*. I had learned to lie spontaneously, without blinking.

Jack shrugged. "See you Wednesday."

I watched him leave. I hated giving up, ever, but this time I might have to. Jack Griffin was making me too uneasy. I had until Wednesday, as far as I could put him off, to work something out. For now, I could forget about him.

And I did.

THIRTEEN

I KNOCKED ON Richard's door a little before nine, weighed down by an old-fashioned wicker picnic hamper that I had salvaged from the utility closet and cleaned up. I couldn't remember the last time I had used it, although from the dust build-up, it could have been as far back as my days with Kirby.

To make the point that I was there to help Jorge, nothing more, I had donned faded jeans and a plain gray sweat shirt.

Richard opened the door wearing faded jeans and a plain gray sweat shirt, and he hadn't shaved.

I took that to mean that he was only there for Jorge, too. I stifled a slight feeling of disappointment.

Richard took the basket, and I followed him into the large kitchen, a clean white room trimmed with blue tile. The refrigerator and stove looked as if they had been installed in the thirties, by the original tenants, and had rarely been used in the intervening years.

Richard uncorked the bottle of wine and took one goblet from a tall cupboard.

"You don't drink?" I asked.

"No. I'm down to caffeine as the last addiction. That one I'm finding hardest to conquer."

"Well, I don't have to drink—"

He lowered his brow in a mock frown.

"If you'd like a glass of wine, have one. You

brought it, and seeing you drink won't bother me. I used to drink. A lot. In fact, I used to wander down to Harrigan's almost every night."

I nodded to let him know I recognized the name, a downtown bar that catered to a mostly professional happy-hour crowd.

"The owners would never let me pay," he said. "I just ran up tabs until I owed them a painting, which they would then hang in the back room. Occasionally they sold one, and they always applied the profit to my tab. I woke up one morning and decided I didn't want to do that anymore."

"Accepting a painting for a bar tab sounds so European. I wouldn't have thought that happened in L.A."

"Oh, yes. They encouraged me to wear paint-spattered clothes, play the artist for the pinstriped masses yearning to breathe free, and I had a good time doing it."

"Then why did you stop?"

He had poured himself a glass of mineral water and added a fat slice of lime. He gestured toward the living room, and I settled down on one of the orchid pillows, where I could look at his painting. It was starting to glow with colors that seemed even more vivid than those of the daytime model outside his window. The night view was a neon fairyland.

"I stopped because some other artists began doing the same thing," he said, once he was seated on the other orchid pillow. "But they abused it, they hawked their paintings in the bar like street vendors, and it wasn't fun any longer."

"Maybe then needed the money more than you did."

"Probably. They also didn't understand that the money comes when you're generous with your work."

"Do you really believe that?"

"Yes."

I shook my head. "I'll have to think about it."

"Why? Don't you give any of your work away?"

"In fact, I do. I'm a therapist, and I give two days a week to a clinic on Sunset."

"A therapist? I would have thought you were some kind of artist."

"Why?"

"Your interest in my work, for one thing. For another, your hands. They're expressive, and you take good care of them. I'm glad you like pale polish."

"Manicures are a cheap way to feel pampered for a few minutes. And I went through the bright purple polish stage, but it was a long time ago."

"Long purple nails must have been distracting to your clients."

"I wasn't a therapist then. I was an actress." I hesitated, not certain what I wanted to tell him. I settled on the truth. "I was on television, a soap for a while, and then a morning talk show. And I started doing a little coke to get up and perky. And somebody decided it was making me unreliable. If I had been a bigger star, if the ratings had been better, I could have survived. But I wasn't and they weren't, so I didn't. So I went to graduate school and started over."

"I understand."

"Do you really?" I shouldn't have had to ask that, but I did.

He nodded. "I've tried most mind-altering substances, both addictive and non, but you can't do them and work—with the possible exceptions of coffee and cigarettes, and I never smoked tobacco. I gave up the rest because I needed to work more than I needed to get high."

"On the subject of drugs—would you mind if we moved the pillows to the other window, so we could watch the street while we talk?"

"Not at all. Especially now that I know how personal this is for you."

I picked up my pillow and walked over to the tall north window. Richard threw his so that it landed next to mine.

"We might as well set up dinner," he said. "You stay, I'll get the tatami mat."

He went to the kitchen and came back with the hamper in one hand, two ceramic hand-fired plates and the necessary flatware in the other, and the mat under his arm.

I picked up the plate he set before me and looked at him questioningly.

"My ex-wife," he said. "A parting gift."

"How long ago?"

"That she left? Five years. We were both young when we got married. I met her in Austria."

"What were you doing in Austria?"

"Traveling. We spent six years traveling around the world together, and then another six in mostly different countries."

"I'm not a good traveler," I said. Then I wished I had said something else, something that hadn't shifted the subject back to me. "Tell me more."

"About what?"

"Anything you want."

Richard thought for a moment, then responded with a long story about an out-of-body experience he had had one night, in which he discussed art with Jackson Pollock and Thomas Hart Benton. I listened, hoping it was a joke.

But the really great thing about it," he said, "was

that I got a chance to ask Pollock if it was true that he had developed his style by watching his father urinate.''

And what did Pollock say?''

"That it was a canard. His father didn't swing his penis when he peed.''

Richard smiled with a little-kid glee. I hadn't expected the line, and I almost choked on the bite of bread in my mouth. I took a sip of wine.

"An artist provocateur, that's what you are,'' I said.

"I hope so,'' he answered.

"What do you think of graffiti as art?''

"Well—it is art, no question of that. And to the extent that it's a life-affirming explosion of color and form, I have to approve of it. I could even approve of it as an expression of anger against the establishment. But most of it is bad art. Most of the tagging is about as aesthetically interesting as the spray of a tomcat. And I have to feel sorry for all those small business owners who are losing their territory to the taggers.''

"Not to mention those of us who have to keep repainting our garage doors,'' I said.

"Your neighbor does that for you, doesn't he? I always see that short, fat man with a paint brush the day after the taggers have visited.''

"That's Norman. His wife has artistic pretensions. I'd love to have your opinion of her work sometime.''

"I don't think I've ever seen her.''

"She almost never leaves the house. When I first moved in, I wondered if she were a vampire, or had that disease that causes people to avoid the sun and gives rise to vampire legends.''

"Does she?''

"Probably not. She's probably just reclusive.''

The conversation continued as we ate. I forgot I was

there to watch the street until my second cup of Cuban coffee. I was reminded by a sound that might have been a gunshot.

I jerked toward the window.

"A backfire," Richard said.

"That car," I said, pointing to a grayish compact of uncertain heritage that was parked a few spaces down the block. I had caught a flash of headlights going out.

There was movement on the sidewalk outside the apartment house gates. Someone had emerged from the shadows of the courtyard and was standing under the streetlight. I had no idea where he had come from or when he had arrived on the scene. I had been distracted by Richard, and I was now annoyed with myself.

The car door slammed.

I was hoping that one of the two men would have red hair, but both of them seemed dark. I couldn't be certain whether they were Anglo or Hispanic.

"Call 911," I said, heading for the apartment door.

"Where are you going?"

"To get a closer look. I have to be able to identify whoever it is."

"Goddamn it, you're nuts!"

"Don't yell at me! Call 911!" I snapped.

I eased the door shut and slipped down the stairs as quietly as I could.

The base of the stairs was still several feet from the sidewalk, and a gingko tree blocked my vision. I took a few careful steps to the tree, staying hidden from the two men by the shadow of the low branches.

The man from the car had his back to me. All I could see was dark hair curling over the collar of a black leather jacket. The man facing me, accepting money, was Hispanic, but no one I recognized from the block.

Their transaction completed, they began to move away from the light.

I had to keep them until the police arrived.

"Excuse me. Could I talk to you?" I blurted it out before I had a chance to be afraid.

I caught a glimpse of a white face before the buyer hurried back to his car. The Hispanic seller stopped and held out his hands. He was young, maybe twenty, with a baby face showing a bare trace of mustache.

"Sorry, mamacita," he said, smiling. "I'm out for the evening. Maybe another time."

"When? When will you be back? Don't leave yet!"

The gray car made a u-turn in the middle of the block behind me, screeching rubber. I whipped around, trying to get another look at the driver's face, but he was gone.

And so was the Hispanic, jogging around the corner.

I started after him, not really wanting to catch him, feeling a little like a dog chasing a car. I wanted to see where he was going, but I didn't make it. He had disappeared by the time I reached the corner.

"Faith!"

Richard was running along the sidewalk behind me.

"What the hell are you doing?"

"Trying to get more information," I said, panting from the combination of exertion and adrenaline.

"Jesus! He could have had a gun!"

"He probably did, but he didn't show it to me. He didn't feel threatened."

I leaned against the closest tree and concentrated on exhaling. If you can get the air out, you can get it back in. One of those handy tricks actors learn in voice class. As my breath stabilized, so did my heartbeat.

"What did the 911 operator say?" I asked, once I could control my voice.

"A car's on the way. I said you were being attacked."

Richard had steadied himself against the wrought iron fence. He wasn't smiling.

"I'll forgive the lie if it gets them here," I said.

"For all I knew, it was the truth. Do you have a death wish or something?"

"I don't think so. But I'll consider the possibility and get back to you."

He sighed and held out his hand. I took it and walked with him back to the apartment.

"Do you mind if I have another glass of wine?" I asked.

"I'll get it for you," he said.

When he returned with it, we sat quietly by the window, watching the street, until the police arrived about ten minutes later.

Page and Davila. Of course, it was Page and Davila.

"That was a hell of a stupid thing to do," Page said, once I had told the story. "You could have been hurt. And suppose he was a murderer—not the one you think you're looking for, but a murderer. Drug dealers aren't your friendly neighborhood beaners. People have gotten themselves killed for a lot less than what you did."

"I only wanted to help. I thought maybe I could delay him until you could get here and pick him up."

"You shouldn't count on a fast response, ma'am," Davila said quietly.

I nodded. I knew that. No one in L.A. should count on a fast response, not ever.

Page snapped his notebook shut.

The goodbyes were reasonably polite all around.

"What do you want to do?" Richard asked, once the two officers had left.

"I think I'd better go home. I have clients coming tomorrow, and I'll only get a few hours sleep as it is."

"Okay. I'll walk with you."

"You don't have to do that."

"Yes, goddamn it, I do." He flared again. "You don't understand how upset I was when I thought you might be hurt."

"No, I guess I don't."

He turned away and started gathering up the remains of the living room picnic.

"That can wait," I told him. "I can retrieve the containers another time."

"Okay. Good." He straightened and turned to me. "That means you're coming back."

"Yes."

This time I held out my hand, and he took it.

We walked down the block to my house in silence. I stopped him on the porch.

"Goodnight."

He leaned down and kissed me. I had known he would, but I hadn't been certain how I would respond. His mouth was hard, his three-day growth scratchy, and I was nervous. Not a promising start.

"I need to go in," I said.

He nodded and walked down the steps, turning when he reached the sidewalk, waiting until I was in the house before proceeding up the street.

I had wanted to be alone to think about Richard, that was true. But I also needed to be alone to think about the glimpse of face, the one I had gotten as the buyer sprinted for his car. It was familiar, I was certain of that. I knew the man. I simply had to bring the rest of the face out of the darkness.

I checked the medicine cabinet, knowing it was in

vain, that there was nothing inside that would calm me down.

And then I had to admit one more thing.

The excitement, the rush, felt good. I felt alive, thrilled, even high. And I wanted the feeling again.

FOURTEEN

"SO WHAT ARE YOU asking us to do?" Alex demanded when I had finished telling the story. The small dragon on his forearm twitched as he took a sip of his Jack Daniels.

I had called a Neighborhood Watch meeting for the following Monday evening, and the group had convened once again in Alex and Wayne's living room. Christopher, Sybil, Ramon, Esteban, Louie, Carol, Martine, and Frieda had all returned. I hadn't asked Michael. Lisa, Graciela, and Richard had enlarged the group to fourteen.

I hadn't talked to Richard in the two intervening days, except for a brief phone call inviting him to the meeting. I felt from his response that I had established some kind of connection with him, though I didn't quite know what it was. And thinking about it made me nervous.

"I'm not really sure what I'm asking," I said, more to the rest of the group than to Alex. "I have no illusions that we can do anything about illegal drugs in Los Angeles—nor that we can even make a dent in what's going on in this neighborhood as a whole. But I think we may be able to stop drug dealing on our block, and some of the crime that comes with it, if we take turns sitting up at night, watching. When you see anything suspicious, call the dispatcher immediately. If we're lucky, the police will get here in time to catch someone in the act. If not, well, if the drug dealers know they're under surveillance here, they'll move somewhere else.''

I looked around, hoping for a response. Nobody moved. Alex gave a snort of disbelief.

''Or maybe we could at least discover some kind of pattern,'' I continued, ''so that the police could set a trap.''

Nothing encouraging happened.

''If we don't do something, the drug-related burglaries are going to continue, and sooner or later somebody else is going to be killed on this block. And next time it could be one of us.'' I couldn't think of anything more to say, so I stopped and waited.

Ramon had been quietly translating for Esteban, who nodded to me at the end of the speech. Everyone else stared at the floor.

''They only kill each other, Faith,'' Christopher finally said. He had worn a long-sleeved T-shirt again, sparing the unwary the sight of his festooned arms. ''As long as we stay out of it, nothing is going to happen to any of us.''

''No,'' Graciela said. ''Jorge stayed out of it, and he is in jail. Something already happened to us. We will stay up and watch.''

''I will watch,'' Frieda said.

Martine frowned, then nodded.

Carol nodded. Ramon half-raised his hand in a gesture that I took to mean that he was volunteering.

''Listen, I know everybody's concerned, especially with the kid from across the street in jail, but don't you think this is getting out of hand?'' Louie asked.

He was sitting on a stool that Alex had dragged in from the kitchen, fidgeting as if he might fall off. With his black shirt and black jeans, and a small black hat on his head, he had almost disappeared, like a Chinese prop man. Louie even had a narrow braid hanging down over his shoulder.

"I mean, is this our business?" he continued. "What somebody else does? It isn't really hurting any of us. This is like a posse, in the movies. I can't believe that any of you want to call the police and have somebody arrested over a private business transaction, and that's what we're talking about, a private business transaction between two consenting adults. Faith, you don't want that. Let them do what they want, if they want to get high, let them just do it."

"Not hurt?" I asked, thinking about the empty space where my stereo had been and how violated I felt when I saw it.

"I can understand that nobody wants people breaking into their homes, but we're talking about what they do on the street. And we don't have any right to interfere with that, do we? Don't we have to pay attention to their rights?"

Everybody waited for me to answer him.

"Louie, I understand what you're saying. I want to defend rights, too. I think we all have them, the people dealing drugs in the street and the people in this room—including life, liberty, and the pursuit of happiness, to borrow a phrase. So I want to defend the rights people have to do what they want as long as they don't interfere with other people's rights. If somebody wants to do drugs in private, they can. As long as they're not interfering with my rights, I won't interfere with them."

I winced at my own rhetoric. I was willing to interfere with Kirby's drug use in private. I plowed on anyway.

"The problem is that drug dealing on the block in front of my house does interfere with my rights, because I believe it was the reason my house was burglarized. A drug user's right to swing his fist stops with my nose, and my nose has been bloodied. And so has Graciela's. And Esteban's. And Jorge's."

"And Alex,'s, and mine," Wayne added.

I was startled at the support. I had forgotten about the earlier burglary. I lost my train of thought.

"Those are things, stereos and VCRs, just things," Louie argued, not caring that the sentiment might be unpopular in that group. "The guys that stole them probably needed them more than you do. Why can't you just let them go?"

"Because it's a violation of my rights," I replied, hoping he could understand. "No one has the right to break into my house and steal my things."

Louie looked down at the carpet.

"So," I said, turning back to Wayne. "Does that mean you want to watch?"

"Yes." Wayne favored me with his sad, Rock-Hudson-as-Confederate-general smile. "We'll take a night."

"Great." I counted heads. "We have six nights covered. Lisa and Carol, Ramon—"

"And my wife," he interjected.

"And his wife. Graciela and Esteban, Wayne and Alex, Frieda and Martine, and me."

"But Faith, you can't see the whole block from your house. You are too far back from the street. And how can you watch all night alone?" Frieda asked.

"I'll work something out," I said. I knew I was blushing, and I couldn't look at Richard.

"I'll take the seventh night," Sybil said.

"I guess I could share it with you," Christopher told her. "One of us early, one of us late. We could call each other."

"Okay. Let's set up a schedule."

I matched volunteers and nights. Louie sulked on his stool. Richard silently blended into the carpet next to the sofa, but everyone else became animated.

Carol, Ramon and his wife, and Wayne turned out to be the only people with straight jobs, so they got Friday, Saturday, and Sunday. Wayne clearly expected Alex to take the late shift Sunday night. Alex went to the kitchen to refill his glass.

Graciela had Tuesday and Sunday off from her housekeeping job, so she and Esteban took Monday night. Frieda and Martine took Tuesday, Christopher and Sybil Wednesday, and I put myself down for Thursday. I still hadn't looked at Richard.

No one had much to say once the schedule was set up and phone numbers exchanged. The excitement ebbed as quickly as it had flowed.

When Lisa stood up and suggested to Carol that they leave, everyone seemed to take that as the end of the evening. Richard, Louie, and I were the last to say goodnight to Wayne. Alex hadn't returned from the kitchen.

"Short meeting," I said, once we were on the porch.

"You can't mean what you said," Louie said, the words bursting out as if he had been holding them for an hour. "If you saw Marcus or me buying drugs, what would you do?"

"If I saw you or Marcus buying drugs, I wouldn't

call the cops," I said, annoyed that he had asked. "You're my friends, and I could talk to you, tell you that I thought it was a lousy idea and ask you to transact business someplace else if you had to buy. But you're right. I couldn't call the cops on you or Marcus."

That was the damn problem. I couldn't call the cops on Kirby, either. I couldn't be Buddy the Narc.

"It's okay somewhere else," Richard said softly, "but not in your backyard."

"Oh, SHIT!" I yelled. "Why am I on the spot? I am goddamn trying to do my best here, for this small piece of humanity, and I can't solve the problems of the whole goddamn world."

I stomped through the gazania, almost tripped over the low retaining wall, and caught my balance just short of Norman's porch. Richard followed, showing a greater respect for the gazania. He dropped a hand on my shoulder as we moved on through a second patch of gazania to the house.

"See you, Faith, and I hope you feel better," Louie called as he headed on to the kitchen door of the house he shared with Marcus.

"It's a tough position," Richard said. "I know that. Have you considered moving?"

"Yes, and I'm not sure I'm ready. Even though I know avoidance works. And thank you for your support."

He kissed me lightly on the mouth. "You're welcome."

"Oh, God, you shaved! I mean, I noticed earlier, but now I really noticed!"

He laughed, a little embarrassed. "You could have

said something Friday, let me know that was important.''

''You're right. I'm sorry. And I'm glad you shaved.''

He kissed me again, searching for a response. This time, it was easier to give.

Amy brushed against my leg.

''I need to feed the cats,'' I said. ''Do you want to come in?''

''Are they twins?'' he asked.

''No, mother and son. But Mac has spent all his life next to Amy, so he never had a chance to individuate properly. I can see why you'd think they were twins.''

The cats trotted through the door as soon as I opened it. I followed them to the kitchen, and Richard followed me.

''Why did Louie come tonight?'' Richard asked, leaning against the door jamb that separated the kitchen from the short, square hall.

''Because it's part of his job as Marcus's houseboy to attend Neighborhood Watch meetings. Marcus has about thirty thousand dollars worth of musical and recording equipment in the back bedroom, and his attitude toward material things and one's right to them is a little different from Louie's.'' I spooned the canned food in a dish. I had learned long ago that it was silly to use two, because Mac always wanted to eat with his mother.

''Does Marcus know he's harboring an anarchist?''

''Probably. And Louie knows that if he doesn't protect Marcus's material things, he won't have a roof over his head.''

I poured a glass of wine for myself and a glass of mineral water for Richard.

"None of this is going to do any good, you know that," Richard said as he took the glass.

"Oh, hell. I don't know that." I moved back to the living room and sat on the couch. Richard sat next to me. "Because if that's true, then I do have to move."

I looked around the room at all my material things. Furniture, plants, books, the beveled antique mirror with its gilded frame, the portrait of my great-grandmother, the hole where the stereo had been.

"Maybe that's why I haven't replaced the stereo, though," I added. "One more thing to pack."

"Give it time. Turn the decision over to your subconscious."

"That should have been my line." I swiveled to face him. He was smiling. "Have you eaten?"

"Not in a while."

"If you want potluck, I could probably manage a salad and an omelet. And there's bread, cheese, and fruit."

"That's what you eat, isn't it? Picnic stuff."

"A lot of the time. I got out of the habit of cooking for myself. I do simple stuff or take-out. You?"

"Pretty much the same. So why don't we go out? The Blue Pearl has open mike poetry readings on Monday night, and a friend of mine is going to be there. I told her I'd try to stop by. The food isn't terrific, but that's not why people go there."

I stiffened, not certain how to react to the idea of his female friend.

"She's a friend," Richard emphasized, catching my tension. "I really do have women friends."

"Good. I have a male friend you can meet sometime. Let's go."

The Blue Pearl was in Venice, and I didn't want to cross the city on his Harley. He agreed to let me drive.

The readings had started at eight. We made it just before nine, and found seats as quietly as we could. The menu was mostly sandwiches, but the smoked mozzarella and sliced tomato with fresh basil on a baguette sounded promising. I ordered that and a decaf latte. Richard ordered the albacore melt and a regular latte.

I made a mental note that he ate fish.

The tables were tiny and crowded, the lights were dim, and the walls were painted black. I wasn't certain it was a place in which I would ever be comfortable. Besides, I was feeling too old and heavy for the thin, mostly twentysomething crowd.

The first reader after we arrived wasn't Richard's friend, but a pale young man whose poems were strings of seemingly disconnected words. I tuned him out and ate my sandwich.

Richard's friend Magdalene was the second reader, a woman barely out of adolescence, with bright orange hair and alabaster skin, dressed in black. Her work at least made sense to me, although the descriptions of casual sex with anonymous men awakened my urge to intervene. I wondered if giving the young poet a business card would be out of line.

The readings continued for about an hour and a half, some intriguing, some embarrassing, at least from my perspective. A man with wiry black hair pulled into a pony tail had joined our table just after Magdalene reached the mike. Richard had whispered an introduction, and I nodded without being certain who the man was.

He turned out to be Magdalene's current boyfriend, Sean.

When Magdalene joined us, all excited about what she perceived as a positive reception—which seemed to mean that no one had booed—we ordered another round of lattes.

Richard and I didn't leave until after midnight.

"How do you do it?" I asked, as I drove the Taurus onto Venice Boulevard, heading back to the Santa Monica Freeway.

"Do what?"

"Drink coffee until all hours, go to sleep, and then get up and work."

"Habit. Just habit. And I don't need more than four hours sleep. That's metabolism."

"I'm wired. I'll never get to sleep."

"Come home with me. Don't face insomnia alone."

"I'm not sure that's a good idea."

"I could prescribe a remedy for sleeplessness, doctor," he said, his tone lightly mocking.

"I'm not a doctor. I have a master's degree and a counselor's license, but I'm not a doctor."

"A shortcut through graduate school?"

"Something like that. Or a consolation prize. I chose to stop with a master's." I wanted to let it go at that, but I couldn't. "I had an affair with a professor, and when he left me, I decided I didn't want to stay. I wasn't going to teach, and I wasn't going to write a book, so one more degree wasn't going to make any difference in my life."

"You don't sound certain of that."

"Well, I am."

"How long ago?"

I remembered asking him that question.

"Almost four years. And I haven't slept with anyone since."

"What? Why not?"

I wanted to look at him, see what expression was in his eyes as he asked, but I had to move to the far left lane for the transition to the Harbor Freeway, a change that always catches me unawares.

"At first I hurt too much," I finally said. "And then I was busy setting up a practice. After that I was sort of out of the habit of dating, and not certain I wanted to get back into it. For what it's worth, though, I'm thinking about it."

"I know." He dropped a hand on my shoulder. "We've both been thinking about it."

I kept my eyes on the traffic.

"And I need to think about it a while longer," I said. "Is that okay with you?"

"I'm not going anywhere. I think I need to tell you that there have been a couple of casual relationships since my divorce. More than a couple. Is that okay with you?"

"Yeah. I guess."

I had to concentrate on the Hollywood Freeway, the Alvarado Street exit.

And then we were in front of my house.

Richard hopped out to open the garage. He waited until I had parked the Taurus, then closed and locked the heavy door.

"We could at least continue the conversation," he said. I hesitated. If I went inside alone, I'd be pacing the floor for hours, even though the lattes had been decaf.

And I didn't want to leave him, not yet.

I hooked my hand inside his elbow, and we walked

up the street to the iron gate, then up the stairs to his apartment.

My heart was beating, and I felt a little of the same rush I had felt when I went running out to confront the drug dealer. The thought tumbled through my head and out again that I had planned to think about the confrontation, sort it out, but with clients on Saturday and a Sunday taken up with making and distributing flyers for the meeting, I had forgotten.

"What can I get you?" Richard asked.

I shook my head. "Unless you have a Valium, I'm fine."

He reached up and ran a finger down the line of my cheek. "More double standard?"

"It wouldn't be if you had a prescription. And I really don't want one."

He kissed me lightly. "Then what?"

"I thought we were going to continue the conversation," I said.

"Fine." He stepped back, arms wide.

I felt as if I had been rational for too long, squelched all my reckless impulses for too many years, and I didn't want to do it any longer.

"Oh, the hell with it," I said. "We've talked enough."

I grabbed his belt buckle and pulled, so that he had to throw his arms around me to regain his balance.

And it turned out that Richard was right about the remedy for sleeplessness. I slept just fine that night.

FIFTEEN

RICHARD'S BEDROOM was a good place to wake up in the morning. The high, uncurtained windows had a southeastern exposure, and sunlight filtered through the lavender blooms of the jacaranda tree.

The bed had turned out to be a futon. A low white dresser was the only other item of furniture in the room. On the wall above the dresser was a black-and-white self-portrait that made sense of the story he had told me, about the astral experience with Benton, and Pollock, clearly both influences on his work. Richard's face was real and smiling and vital, almost as if transferred from a photograph, and the background was black spatters on the white canvas.

I eased myself onto an elbow, wanting to take a moment to look at him while he slept. Softened lines, what happens to bodies when they are no longer young. He was lean, though, and his skin was that rich color that artists call flesh, and his muscles had definition.

But the line of his shoulder, of his back, was gentle, and his hair fell easily into the hollow of his neck. I couldn't see his face.

I settled down next to him, and the movement woke him up.

He rolled over and blinked. "How are you?"

"Terrific. And you?"

"Every man is twenty-three in the morning."

He was wrong, of course. Twenty-three-year-olds are in a hurry. Richard was old enough to take his time.

By the time I was able to unglue myself from his body and crawl to the bathroom, the sun was well up.

Like the kitchen, the bathroom was white tiles with dark blue trim. I did my best to get rid of old makeup with soap and water and one of the dark blue towels.

Richard had coffee ready when I returned to the bedroom. He had put on his faded jeans and was almost bouncing on his bare toes.

"I hate to say this, but I want to work today," he said, handing me a mug. "I am overflowing with the need to work. But I'd like to see you soon."

"Me, too. And I know I didn't ask you first, but—"

"But Thursday night is your night to watch, and you can't see much of the street from your house."

"Well, yeah."

"Thursday night it is."

I got dressed, finished my coffee quickly, and left. The morning was a little too bright, and I had forgotten my dark glasses. But my heartbeat was easy.

When I got home, the need to share the excitement was irresistible. I had to call Michael.

"What are you doing up so early?" he asked.

"I spent the night with Richard. I thought you'd want to know."

"Congratulations. I'm thrilled for you. That explains the energy in your voice. Forget that theory that the British built an empire on repressed sexuality, or that energy spent on sex is lost forever. Energy spent on lousy relationships is probably lost forever, but that put into good ones—even incipient good ones—comes back in the morning tenfold. What are you going to do with this wonderful day?''

''Get to the clinic on time. And tomorrow I have to clean house.''

''Oh my God, the nesting instinct kicking in. You must have had a good night.''

''I did, but wanting to clean has nothing to do with nesting. I simply want order and beauty around me. The aesthetic instinct, perhaps. And I know you won't like this, but I have to call Kirby. This is the end, truly, and I have to let him know. And this is therefore my last chance—his last chance—for an intervention.''

''Good luck.'' Michael barely paused before he said it.

''I know you don't approve, and I'm sorry. I have to do it anyway.''

''Yes, and I understand. And I know I shouldn't have to ask this, but I'm going to anyway. Your new friend does understand about safe sex, doesn't he?''

''Yes, and so do I, and thank you for asking.''

''Changing the subject from sex, which I have to do when I'm only thinking about it and have been that way for some time, have you figured out how to get the boy out of jail?''

''Not quite.'' I brought him up to date on the Neighborhood Watch.

''This is even more dangerous than sleeping with men you hardly know,'' Michael said when I was through. ''Instant death. There must be a better way.''

''Call me when you think of it,'' I replied.

''I will.''

Before putting down the phone, I called Kirby. I knew he wouldn't answer this early in the morning, but I left a message on his machine.

"Dinner tonight or tomorrow. Let me know."

The energy from the night carried me through the day at the clinic, including the apologies for having missed the week before, but I was starting to flag a little when I got home. And Kirby had left a message in response.

"Tonight, madame. I'll see you tonight at eight."

I tried to be on time, but I ended up fifteen minutes late, the best balance I could reach between the desire to avoid the confrontation and the need to attempt an intervention.

"Aha!" Kirby cried as I reached the front door. "You're finally here! I've been pacing, worried. You're never late."

"I'm often late. You don't notice because you're usually later."

I stopped just outside his reach. I didn't want him to touch me. Part of it had to do with Richard, and the knowledge that even after all these years, Kirby would see what had happened as infidelity. I wished that I had said a final goodbye to Kirby first.

My eyes filled, and I blinked back tears.

"Yes, stand there, with the edge of the light touching your hair. Your beauty beggars description, madame."

"I loved you so much, Kirby."

He smiled, but the smile was ragged. He knew I didn't want to be touched, and that made me feel worse.

And I wondered how I had failed to notice how ravaged his eyes were, that first night at Marcus's party. The damage had to have been there then—it couldn't have happened in a week and a half.

"Would you like to come in?" he asked.

I shook my head.

He nodded.

I turned and started back up the steps, not waiting for him to follow. I kept just ahead of him, all the way to the garage. He flicked the door open with the remote, and I waited while he backed the Jaguar out.

"Henri's?" he asked.

"Of course."

It should end where it began.

We rode down the hill in silence.

We spoke as necessary to get out of the car and into the restaurant, to walk to the table, to order the wine and the meal.

When the waiter had poured the wine, Kirby lifted his glass and said, "Here's to the end, my only friend."

"I won't drink to that."

"Then I'll drink to it alone."

He drank half the glass in one gulp.

I tried to think of a toast to counter with, but I couldn't. I set the glass down untouched.

"You wanted to talk," he said. "Talk."

"I really want you to talk," I answered. "I tried to figure out why dinner with your parents was so difficult for you, and all I could come up with was Dixie talking about work. And me talking about work. And Chas talking about work. And you weren't. What's happening with your career?"

"Oh, hell, you know the industry, all a bunch of assholes."

"*Outgunned* came out last year, so you must have shot it the year before. You must have something new going on."

"Is this a talk or a fucking inquisition?"

"How about a recording deal? Got a contract for a new CD?"

"I'm not ready to go into a studio yet, that's all. I can have a new contract any time I want one. Now back off." His eyes had narrowed, his voice hardened.

I moved to another tack.

"A couple of days ago I ran into a friend of yours, from Madison High. Bill Zaslov."

"Jesus. Bill Zaslov. I remember him. What's he doing?" Kirby seized the name, hoping I had changed the subject.

"Getting underprivileged kids to achieve, that's what he's doing."

"He's practically a saint. Like you. You should have gotten together with him in college, not with me." He paused, then slammed his empty glass down. "Wait— that's what this is about! Bill Zaslov! Somebody else! You want me to know that you're involved with somebody else!"

"No, goddamn it, no. That's not what this is about!"

I was blushing, and I knew he thought I was lying.

"I can see it in your face," Kirby said, "which will never again turn to me at midnight with a sigh."

"Thank you, Edna!" I snapped.

The waiter arrived with the salads. He refilled Kirby's glass and left.

Neither one of us picked up a fork.

"I met Bill Zaslov to talk about Jorge Carrasco," I continued, "the boy arrested for murder. And Bill remembered me from the university, and remembered that I knew you. He said to say hello. He remembered what a tremendous talent you were, and I was glad he did, because I was beginning to think I had it all wrong."

"I haven't done all that badly. I'm not teaching high school, and I haven't quit and walked away from a good career for a second-rate nothing one as a so-called therapist.''

''What does that mean?''

''Just watch who you're calling a failure.'' Kirby drank another half glass.

''I didn't use that word,'' I said, confidence draining from my voice.

''I remember you, too, and what talent you had. You could act, you could write, and you were smart. You could have been another Barbara Walters, if that's what you'd wanted—if you'd fought back and gone for it when you lost the *Coffee Break* show. Everybody gets cancelled. Not everybody gives up because of it. But you did. You walked away. That's what you've done all your life, walk away. That's why you've never married. You can't handle commitment. And now you're walking away from me, and saying it's my fault. No, madame. This time the failure is not mine.'' The words had come out as if on one long breath.

''This is not about failure. I wasn't calling you a failure.'' I stopped to gain control of myself. Every time I thought I had laid those personal demons, success and failure, to rest, one popped up again to laugh at me. ''And it isn't about us, or me. I have some empathy for what's happening to you because I did snort my television career right up my nose and then I didn't have whatever it took to try again. But you're not simply blowing your career. What can I say to make you realize that if you don't stop what you're doing, you'll end up as dead as Tigger?''

''Of course I'll end up as dead as Tigger. We'll all end up as dead as Tigger. Is that what you wanted to talk about? Death? I know death, madame, and I know grief, and when death comes, I will welcome her.''

"Oh, God, that's what you're doing, isn't it? Slow suicide. And you know it." I looked at his face, and a dead man looked back. "Get help, Kirby. Please get help. I can't help you, but somebody can. The people who love you know grief, too."

"Excuse me."

The tables at Henri's were close together. Kirby hit the one next to us so hard that he overturned the flowers as he pushed his way out. The woman grabbed the vase, catching it neatly before it landed. The waiter was there immediately with a cloth, apologizing profusely to the well-dressed couple who had almost gotten a wet dinner.

"I'm sorry, too," I said. "Could you please bring the check and package our dinners to go? I don't think we'll be able to stay after all."

The waiter nodded. The woman at the table smiled in sympathy. Her partner shook his head and chuckled.

"Some guys shouldn't drink," he said.

I smiled and nodded.

When Kirby returned, he saw the two white foam containers sitting on the table. He clicked his heels together and bowed.

"Whenever you're ready."

I picked up the dinners and led the way out.

We were silent while the valet brought the Jaguar, and we rode in silence to Kirby's house. I got out quickly once the car was in the garage.

"I think this one's yours," I said, holding out a container.

"Please keep them both. You paid for them."

"Kirby, this is not what I wanted."

"Nor is it what I wanted. But it seems to be what we have."

He licked his fingers, stuck them in his nose, and sniffed. Bad timing.

"Please get help," I said. "I wish I could help you, but I don't know how."

He smiled, that awful, ragged, haunted smile.

"Then you have to leave, don't you?"

"Yes. Goddamn you, yes, I do."

I turned on my heels and stomped to the car, not looking back. I dropped the dinners and my purse on the floor of the passenger side and screeched rubber pulling away from the curb.

Too angry to go home, I picked up the Golden State Freeway north and drove all the way to the Magic Mountain exit, gas pedal to the floor, before I was calmed down enough to remember the speed limit. And by then I was crying. I stopped on the overpass until my tears were dry.

"Goodbye, Magic Mountain," I whispered, and turned toward the southbound ramp.

By the time I reached the Alvarado Street exit from the Hollywood Freeway, it was almost eleven. Time to accept that Kirby had set me free fifteen years ago, and I would have to set myself free now.

I was about to turn toward the garage door when my headlights picked up two men at the end of the block, just beyond the glow of the streetlight.

This was supposed to be Frieda and Martine's night to watch. I wasn't certain they could see that far, or make out figures standing outside the circle of light.

I thought about what Kirby had said, that I couldn't make a commitment. I thought of what I had said to Louie, that if I saw him buying drugs I would try to talk to him about it. And I thought about the rush I had felt five nights earlier, when I had confronted the baby-faced drug dealer.

One of the men was dark, maybe baby-face, one seemed to be a redhead.

I drove the car slowly toward them. I caught a glimpse of a white face, not baby-face, the same cheek, the same profile I had seen there before. But this time I knew who it was.

A car backed out of a driveway immediately in front of me. I had to slam on the brakes to avoid hitting it. And my engine died. The strange car stayed there, blocking my path. No one got out.

I turned the ignition key, but the engine didn't catch. Nervously, I had kept my foot on the gas. Flooded. I had flooded the engine.

"You again, mamacita? What is it you're looking for?"

The baby-faced drug dealer was standing next to the car.

"I thought we could talk," I said. "I thought if I could find out what was going on here, understand the situation, maybe we could help each other out."

"Help each other out?"

"Yes." I was feeling the rush again. I waited until it was under control before I continued. "You could tell me your story. I'm a good listener."

"What for? You want to put me on television?"

"No. I used to interview people for television, but I don't anymore."

"Oh, yeah? You were on television? Really?"

"Yes. Really. A few years ago."

He looked at me, looked away.

"So what is it you want to know?"

"About you. As much as you'll tell me, who you are, what you do."

"Now?"

"Why not?"

He pondered. "I can't tell you my name—not so anybody could find me."

"Okay." My heart was pounding. I wondered if anyone had called the police.

"But you could call me Salvador."

"Fine. Salvador. Is that where you're from?"

"Yeah. I come here three years ago, with my brothers, looking for work. But we couldn't find it. It is not my fault I am dealing drugs, you know? And now one of my brothers is dead."

"That was your brother? The young man who was killed in the street here?"

"Yeah, that was my brother. But no one cares, you know? There is no one to mourn him except my little brother and me."

"I'm sorry. That must be very hard for you. Do you have any idea who killed him?"

"No, he was here alone. Just making a drop for an Anglo. If I knew the killer, I would go after him."

"The Anglo—is that the redhead?"

"No. He is a regular customer, the redhead, but not that night. The Anglo is a rich kid, he buys for his friends. I have lots of rich kid customers."

Salvador was getting restless.

"There's a young man in jail for killing your brother," I said. "The police think it was some sort of gang-related murder."

"The cops are so dumb." He shook his head. "Someone just ripped my brother off, that's all. He was carrying high-grade stuff, you know? Straight from Colombia. And somebody wanted what he had and killed him for it.''

''All right! Don't move! I've got a gun, and the police are on their way!''

I froze. The voice was Wayne's.

Salvador didn't freeze. He turned and fired four shots in succession. I hadn't even noticed that he was holding a gun.

Now it was turned on me.

''You did this, lady? You set me up?''

''No, I didn't. I wanted to talk to you, I hoped I could convince you to move your operation somewhere else, and I wasn't expecting anyone, not anyone with a gun.'' My adrenaline rush went into overload, contorting my face with fear, and I could barely get my mouth to work. Sweat was pouring down my armpits.

''Okay. I don't like to kill women, you know? So I'm gonna believe you. But maybe you owe me, and maybe I come back for you.''

The driver of the car blocking the street yelled, ''Come on, we gotta get out of here.''

Salvador got in and they peeled away. One red tail light stared at me like a dragon's eye until the car turned the corner.

I still couldn't move.

A man was screaming somewhere, wounded animal screams.

Lights were coming on. People were shouting.

I was whimpering, funny little choked crying sounds, and I couldn't let go of the steering wheel.

Then somebody shook me. My neck snapped back and forth, and I managed one good wail.

I was pulled from the car, and then I was sobbing

into a sweat shirt. I recognized the smell of Richard's body.

"It's all right, baby," he said, stroking my hair.

I knew it wasn't all right, and I didn't want to face whatever had happened.

But I lifted my head from Richard's chest anyway.

The patrol car was parked just down the block, lights on. Page was inside, talking to someone on the radio. Davila was talking to Alex, who was standing on the pavement in his bathrobe, sobbing. Christopher had an arm around him.

Sybil was standing on one side of the street. Carol and Lisa, Ramon and his wife, Esteban and Graciela were scattered down the other side.

I looked for Wayne and didn't see him.

There was a heap on the pavement with a coat thrown over it. Dark rivulets had run from it, tiny lines of wetness, shining in the headlights.

Alex turned and saw me staring.

"This is your fault!" he cried. "Wayne's dead, and it's your fault!"

SIXTEEN

I WOKE UP in Richard's bedroom, sun streaming through the windows and bouncing off the white walls. I shut my eyes, not willing to deal with so much brightness, and felt for his body. I was alone on the futon.

Something wasn't right. I couldn't remember making love the night before. In fact, I couldn't remember how I got there, or anything about the night before. I felt my head, but it didn't ache. No hangover. I poked around for the memory.

And found it. I had wanted to forget, but it was there.

Salvador, the baby-faced drug dealer, had shot Wayne. And it was my fault. Alex had screamed at me until I was numb.

Page had taken my statement, then calmly and thoroughly chewed me up and spit me out for my senseless behavior.

Richard had put my car in the garage and brought me here.

I curled up into a tight fetal position and buried my face in the pillow. I wanted a cat to hug, and I didn't want to deal with another human being. Ever. I felt unworthy to interact with human beings.

Richard's bare feet padded across the floor to the bed.

"I could make coffee," he said quietly. "And we could talk about it."

I dug deeper into the pillow.

"Hiding isn't going to help. And Alex was wrong—it wasn't your fault."

"Yes, it was," I said into the pillow.

"I can't hear you."

I moved my face from the pillow to his thigh.

"It was my fault. I thought I could talk to him and somehow work this out. Wayne thought I was in trouble. And I was the one who had urged everyone to watch the street."

"That's true. But you didn't know Martine was going to get binoculars, so she could see details at the end of the block."

"She got binoculars? I missed this part."

"Yeah. And Frieda let her have the front bedroom during her watch, and she was all excited when she saw what was apparently a drug transaction going on. She called the police, and then she saw you drive up. And she saw that the dealer had a gun. So she called Wayne, because she was frightened, and she didn't know what else to do."

"See?" I moaned. "It was my fault. Did Wayne really have a gun?"

"Yeah. A service revolver. He was a retired military lifer, did you know that?"

"No, I didn't. How do you?"

"I listened to Alex give Page his statement while you were in shock last night. Wayne had a distinguished career. They didn't know he was gay. You were there when Alex said it, but I didn't think you heard."

"I didn't. And it doesn't make me feel any better."

"It should. I'm telling you that you weren't the only one who miscalculated. Wayne did, too. You both underestimated the enemy because he looked like a kid. Probably is a kid. And you could be just as dead as Wayne is."

"But I'm not."

"Do you wish you were?"

I had to think about it.

"No. I'm glad I'm alive. And that makes me feel even worse."

Richard rubbed the back of my neck.

"Survivor's guilt. It's a bitch, isn't it?"

"Yeah. And don't forget it was my fault he was there at all."

"Was it your fault Salvador was dealing drugs on this block? Was it your fault Wayne and Alex were robbed by a dope fiend?"

"Dope fiend?" I sat up.

"Whatever." He smiled at my reaction.

"No. That wasn't my fault."

"You and Wayne both did something reckless because you were both burglarized for drug money and both wanted to get the dealer off this block. Wayne got killed. You could have been killed."

I didn't say anything. I remembered how the rush of excitement had turned to terror.

"Suppose it had been Wayne's night to watch," Richard said, "the night he had volunteered to watch, and you hadn't been around, and he had run out there and been killed. Would you have felt responsible?"

"Yes."

"That's a heavy load. How far does it extend—just your neighbors, just the block, the city of L.A.? The country? The world? How do you expiate your guilt for the destruction of the Brazilian rain forests when you, after all, live in the same country that houses the multinationals responsible for it?''

''I don't eat beef.''

''But you wear leather shoes, and that big black bag is made from a cowskin.''

''The cow it came from died of old age in Iowa. I asked the saleswoman, and she swore on her mother's grave.''

''Does that mean a practical approach to guilt is possible?''

''I'm not sure. I'll have to think about it.''

I was starting to feel better, even though I didn't think I should. And I had to get up to use the bathroom. I decided I could make it.

''Coffee?''

''Yes, thank you.'' I kissed his unshaven cheek.

I wasn't ready to get dressed, because that meant putting back on the sweat-stained rose silk blouse and white pants that I had worn for dinner with Kirby the night before. I picked up Richard's bathrobe, the faded gray flannel he had been wearing when I first knocked on his door. The robe smelled good and felt right.

The problem with using a man's bathroom is always the lack of moisturizer. I scrubbed the old makeup off my face, which was shiny and dry when I reached the living room.

''How are you doing?'' Richard asked. He was sitting on a pillow with two mugs of coffee beside him on the low table.

''Better. Thanks.''

I took one of the mugs.

''What are your plans for the day?'' he asked.

I looked at the painting, saw how much work he had

done, and knew he wanted to work. Even under stress, maybe especially under stress, he wanted to work. He also wanted me to be all right about it.

"I have to go to the police station and see if I can find Salvador in their mug shots." I had discussed that with Page the night before, and I remembered.

Richard nodded.

"And I want to talk with Miriam Stern, to see if any of this might help get Jorge out of jail."

"Good." His relief was obvious.

"I'd better get dressed," I said.

I took my coffee to the bedroom. When I returned to the living room, ready to leave, he was studying the painting.

"I'll talk to you later."

"Oh." He was startled out of his concentration. "Yeah. And we're still on for tomorrow night, whether we watch the block or not. Nine o'clock. And I'll fix dinner this time."

"Thanks again." I walked over and put my arms around him, leaning against his back.

He turned and kissed me lightly.

"See you."

I walked the short block home wondering about calling off the watch, or if it existed anymore no matter what I did. Wayne was dead, and Salvador wasn't likely to come back.

And I had other things to think about.

Tigger had died from pure Colombian. Salvador said his brother had been carrying pure Colombian, going to meet an Anglo. The fact that he had been wearing my jacket when he died suggested that he might have met someone else, too, because there was no reason for a dealer to burglarize my house. But the Anglo buyer was a place to start.

And I'd had a glimpse of a face the night before, a glimpse of the Anglo making the buy. I was almost certain it was Gordo. Maybe Gordo had bought the Colombian that killed Tigger, given it to Kirby with a warning that Kirby hadn't passed on. I had to talk to him.

I pounded on Marcus's door. The stereo was on, so he was up.

"Hey, girl," Marcus said, when he finally opened it. "What's happening?"

He was half-clad in sweat pants again. I shook away the strange intimacy of neighbors, the bathrobes and sweat pants, the semi-nudity with semi-strangers.

"You heard about last night?"

"I did. Tragedy has struck one more time, hitting those close to us. And we have been fortunate again, that we were spared. Gimme a kiss."

He held out his cheek and I pecked it.

"I need to get in touch with a trombone player named Gordon Wells, known as Gordo. He plays a lot with Kirby McKenzie, but I don't want to call Kirby for the number. Do you have it?"

"I might. Come on in while I check my Rolodex."

I waited in the kitchen until he returned, piece of paper in hand.

"This is the number I have for him. It's old, though, and I don't know if it's good. A little blow for recreational purposes is one thing—I've done it myself. But guys that have heavy habits, like Kirby and Gordo and some of the dudes they hang out with, get unreliable. If Kirby shows up at a party and wants to play, that's fine. Same with Gordo or any of the others. But I wouldn't want any of them around on a gig.''

''If Kirby isn't getting work, he has family resources to fall back on. What about Gordo?''

''I don't know, girl. You'll have to ask him.''

Denise wandered into the kitchen wearing a slip.

''Hi, Faith. I thought I heard your voice.''

''Hi, Denise. I was just leaving.''

I wiggled my fingers at them both and backed out the door.

Amy and Mac were waiting on the porch.

''I'm sorry,'' I said. ''And I can't handle any more guilt.''

After I fed the cats, I retreated to my office and tried the number.

An answering machine picked up, with Gordo's voice on the tape, asking me to leave a message. I didn't. I hung up and called Miriam Stern.

She listened to the story, not responding until the end. Her voice was low and tired.

''I'm sorry about your neighbor,'' she said. ''I really am. And I hope you'll stop acting like a crazy woman now. Let the police take it. I am grateful that you've been willing to help Jorge, but you've done enough.''

''And my neighbor got killed because I was doing it.''

''Hey—you didn't kill him. Salvador did, and the police have to go after him.''

''Will this create enough doubt about the murder that the police will release Jorge?''

''Probably not. But the preliminary hearing is Monday, and your testimony, plus the wavering eyewitness, may convince the judge that there isn't enough evidence to bring Jorge to trial. Then he'll be free. That would be best case. Worst case, he'll get out on bail.''

"What time Monday?''

"Meet me in my office at nine, and we'll walk over together.''

"See you then.''

I took the time to shower and change before leaving for the police station. A last glance in the mirror told me that even though I had done my best, the stress was taking a toll.

And the discovery that the interior of my car stank of decaying food thanks to the contents of the two foam cartons on the floor destroyed the little bit of good feeling I had been trying to nurture. I dumped the uneaten dinners in the garbage.

The next hour didn't help. I spent it looking at pictures, sitting at a desk in a small room near the detectives' area. My eyes hurt and I wanted to cry. But then I spotted the one I wanted to see.

"That's Salvador,'' I said. "That's the one who shot Wayne.''

"Are you positive?''

Detective Ryder was tall, bald, rumpled, and friendly, with sandy sideburns and a sandy mustache. I was relieved that at least I didn't have to deal with Page any longer.

"Positive.''

"Let me run him through the computer and see what I come up with.''

I took off my glasses and shut my eyes. I could still see the baby-faced monster, with his large, dark, innocent eyes meeting mine. His eyes had looked innocent even after he coolly shot Wayne.

Detective Ryder was only gone a moment before returning with a printout.

"Miguel Tejeda," he read. "Twenty years old. Juvenile record sealed. Pleaded guilty to one felony count of possession after he turned eighteen, served one year of a three-year sentence, out on parole. I guess I don't need to tell you this is a violation of his parole."

"But he told me he had only been in the country three years. How could he have a juvenile record?"

"He lied. He and his two brothers grew up in East L.A. Only one has a record. We can check to see if the kid who was killed two weeks ago was the other one."

"But he hasn't been reported missing?"

Ryder shrugged.

"Is there anything more I can do?" I asked.

"Yes. Stay out of the street. Next time he might kill you."

I nodded meekly and said goodbye.

My car still smelled stale.

It was almost noon by the time I got home. When I tried Gordo's number, he answered.

"Can I meet you somewhere?" I asked. "To borrow a phrase, can we talk?"

Gordo laughed. "Sure. I was just thinking about breakfast. How about Puerto Vallarta in half an hour?"

I tried to remember the last time I had eaten. My stomach gurgled at the thought.

"Good idea. See you."

Puerto Vallarta was a small restaurant in Echo Park that served breakfast twenty-four hours a day, and it had long been a favorite musicians' hangout for that reason.

I thought about huevos rancheros as I drove east on Sunset. A cup of Mexican chocolate. Rice and beans.

Guacamole. I hoped that nothing Gordo said would ruin my appetite.

A silent waitress in a red peasant blouse and black skirt pointed out a booth in the back and nodded when I said I was expecting a friend.

I had been waiting about ten minutes, alternately reading the menu and staring at the mural of Central American farm life that worked its way around the interior of the dimly lit restaurant, when Gordo arrived.

He kissed my cheek and sat down on the dark red plastic seat across from me. He didn't pick up a menu. Fresh tortilla chips and salsa appeared immediately.

"Thanks, Loretta," he said.

The silent waitress nodded and turned to me.

"She knows what I want," Gordo added.

"What?" I asked.

"Scrambled eggs and chorizo, flour tortillas, rice and beans, coffee. I come in a couple of times a week."

"I'll have huevos rancheros, corn tortillas, and a cup of chocolate." I stuck my glasses back in my purse.

I watched the waitress walk to the kitchen. There was something stately in Loretta's gait, as if she had been born a princess and had never lost the aristocratic carriage.

Gordo was smiling, a thin smile in a pale face, waiting for me to say something.

"How long have you and Kirby been friends?" I asked.

"Since seventh grade. He was the first friend I made when my parents moved to L.A."

"From where? And why?"

"From Omaha. Because my father was an engineer, and he decided L.A. was the place to be. And he was right, except not in engineering. When he was laid off six years later, he became a real estate agent and never looked back.''

''Not even in the downturn?''

''He grumbled. But he made a pile in the eighties, and he didn't spend it.''

''What about your mother?''

''She never liked L.A., never got over the move. The only friend she made was Jim Beam. Why are you asking?''

''Curious.'' I smiled. Or tried to, anyway. ''I've known you for almost twenty years, and I don't really know much about you.''

''That's because we only knew each other through Kirby. We've never been alone before.''

''That's true, isn't it?'' I was embarrassed. I hadn't thought of it that way.

Obviously Gordo had. He reached across the table and took my hand.

''I know you can't go back to Kirby, babe, if that's what you want to tell me.''

Loretta arrived with coffee and chocolate, allowing me an opportunity to extricate my hand. My smile felt stretched and nervous.

''You're right, of course. I can't go back to Kirby. But I still care about him, and I'm worried. I'm hoping you can help him. He's doing way too much dope, and he was terribly upset over Tigger's death. I think he may feel responsible.'' I sipped the chocolate. So far, so good. I was still hungry.

''Sure he's upset. I'm upset, too. But what makes you think he feels responsible?''

''Well—when he said Tigger didn't know how pure the cocaine was, I thought maybe Kirby knew and could have warned him.''

Breakfast appeared. Gordo smiled at Loretta, who left silently.

"You think Kirby gave him the blow?"

"Do you?"

Gordo buttered a tortilla, filled it with rice and beans, added a little salsa, and rolled it up, before he answered.

"No. There hasn't been much pure stuff around, and if Kirby had any, he would have shared it with me. Wherever Tigger got it, it wasn't from Kirby."

I had no idea whether he was lying. The session with Salvador had destroyed my confidence in my own instincts.

"Or from you?" I asked.

"Or from me."

He was eating so calmly that I picked up my fork and cut into the sauce-laden eggs.

"But you do agree that Kirby is doing too much dope."

"Kirby's an addict, Fay. Nobody's denying that, not even Kirby."

I didn't tell him that Kirby had denied it to me.

"Then why doesn't somebody do something about it?" I asked.

"Who? What?"

"I don't know. He won't listen to me. And I talked to Dixie, and she won't listen to me."

"What did you want her to do?"

"Throw him into rehab. That's what I wanted her to do. Or someone to do."

"He doesn't want to go. And as long as he doesn't want to go, no one can make him, not even Dixie. He wants to keep doing what he's doing, music and blow. That's his life."

"And he's going to keep doing it until he dies."

That stopped Gordo, but only for a moment.

"Probably."

"How do you handle it, losing one friend and watching another die slowly?"

That stopped him a little longer. He put his fork down and took a sip of his coffee.

"First, I don't think I am responsible for either one of them, so I don't take their deaths personally. Second, I figure we all die sooner or later, and if it makes Kirby happy to have me over there playing while he's alive, that's what I'm going to do."

"He isn't working anymore, is he?"

"No. He hasn't worked in months, although he keeps talking about cutting another CD."

"What about you?"

"I work about as much as I always did, an occasional studio gig here or there. What is it you really want to ask me? What's happening that's made you so jumpy?"

I was annoyed at the question. I thought I had been calm and casual. But since I hadn't been, I decided to tell him the whole story, starting with Marcus's party and the death in the street.

"So I want to know if you buy from Miguel Tejeda or his brothers," I finished. "I want to know if it was you I saw either night."

"You want to know if I've been buying drugs in front of your house, where the kid who burglarized your house was murdered."

"Yes. Or up the block."

Gordo shook his head, laughing quietly. "Has it occurred to you that this whole problem, this whole mess, has happened because selling and using cocaine is illegal? And that drives the price up? And makes Kirby and me—and you—and probably half the people you know criminals?''

''It has occurred to me. And I try not to think about it, because I can't take that one on. If I could somehow vote to decriminalize cocaine, and marijuana, and even heroin, and put the money being wasted chasing down small-time dealers and users into rehab programs, I would do it in an instant. I would have voted to repeal Prohibition, too, the way the rest of the country did when they realized that some behavior can be successfully outlawed, but some can't. So far, though, there hasn't been much effort to decriminalize beyond the push for medicinal use, and I can't devote my life to that particular cause.''

''That's fair. I can't, either.''

''You haven't answered my question.''

''Why are you asking me?''

''I told you. I think the man I saw in the street may have been you.''

''Suppose it was. Would you then conclude I murdered somebody? And that I'm going to sit here and tell you about it?'' He shook his head. ''We've known each other a long time, but not that long.''

''Goddamn it, you do know something! I could—'' I didn't finish, because I couldn't.

''Call the cops? What would you say? That I killed somebody? I didn't. That you think I might have been in the street—but you're not sure—and that I might have some information that I won't give you? They might or might not act on that.'' He softened his tone and smiled at me again. ''What you probably could do is get them to go after me for possession. If they knocked on my door with a warrant, they might catch me with something. Do you want to do that?''

''No.'' Buddy the Narc. ''What if I got Jorge's attorney to subpoena you?''

''Lawyers don't like witnesses when they don't know what the witness might say. I could get up on a stand and swear I saw an argument between two men over a deal, and one of them knifed the other, and identify Jorge as the guy with the knife. You don't know.''

I had managed to eat most of my food as we talked. Which was fortunate, because I was losing my appetite.

''You swear to me that you didn't do it?''

''I swear.''

''But you know who did.''

''I didn't say that.''

''Could you get Jorge off?''

''Who knows?'' He shrugged. ''The cops arrest who they want to arrest, convict who they want to convict. They may let him go without my testimony. When's the preliminary hearing?''

''Monday.''

''Why don't you give me a call afterwards? Let me know how it goes.''

Gordo was smiling at me again.

''Okay. I can do that.'' I made an effort to smile back.

Gordo looked around for Loretta, caught her eye, and held up his coffee cup.

''I have to go,'' I said.

I pulled out my wallet, but Gordo caught me.

''On me. Please.''

''Okay. Thanks.''

I tried to sort out what Gordo had said as I drove

home. Denial is the favorite defense of addicts, whatever the drug of choice. Alcohol, cocaine, work, sex. Nobody wants to admit that dependence is ruining life. And co-dependents are the people who help maintain the illusion that life is still okay, by helping them deny the ruin.

I had been a user—an abuser—who never quite got caught in the downward spiral of addiction. I had stopped in time, but only because I left television and started graduate school. Only the change in scenery and lifestyle kept me within the bounds of what I could only charitably describe as social use. Not everyone makes those changes, for one reason or another.

And as I discovered that first night with Kirby, the part of me that was vulnerable to cocaine years ago was only in hibernation. It hadn't died.

Addicts are really good at surrounding themselves with mothers, friends, and other helpers. Sometimes ex-lovers. Gordo may or may not be an addict himself, but he was certainly Kirby's co-dependent. And I had been, too, a long time ago. I didn't want to think about how many years Kirby had been on the long slide down. He just had farther to fall than most people.

If Gordo knew something, if he was protecting someone, the most probable choice was Kirby. I also didn't want to think about what Gordo might be protecting him from.

I turned the corner of the block and saw Jack Griffin standing on my front porch.

"What is he doing here today?" I asked aloud.

And answered my own question. I had told him to come on Wednesday. I had planned to have a referral ready. And I had let him fall through the cracks of my life.

SEVENTEEN

THE HUEVOS RANCHEROS churned in my stomach. I had to concentrate to keep them there.

"Where the hell have you been?" Jack Griffin shouted when I got out of the car to open the garage door.

"I'm sorry. Let me put the car away. I'll be right there."

Once the car was inside, I sat there, shifting mental gears away from the situation with Gordo and Kirby to deal with this man and my own failure to do the job I had trained for and was now being paid for.

When I was as calm as I was going to get, I got out of the car, pulled the garage door shut, and met him on the steps.

"Let's sit on the porch for a moment," I said.

"I don't want to sit on the porch. And I want to know what happened!" His face was red and his fists were clenched.

"We're not going inside," I said calmly. "I cannot take your money any longer. I cannot continue this course of therapy. I am not the right person for you to see, and I hope you will accept my referral to someone better able to deal with you."

"I don't want a referral! I want to talk to you! What the hell is this?"

"Please sit," I said.

He sat down beside me, breathing heavily.

"I'm sorry, Jack," I said, when his breath became more even. "I really am. But I'm not comfortable with what I sense is barely repressed violence in you. I think you need to talk with a man about it, or a woman more comfortable with violence, less inclined to perceive it as a personal threat. This is my failure, not yours."

"What—you thought I was going to hit you?"

"There have been moments when the thought crossed my mind, yes."

"I've never hit Linda. Why would I hit you?"

"I don't know. And that makes it my problem, not yours." I pulled a notebook and pen out of my bag and scribbled down a name and telephone number. "This man is a professor of clinical psychology. I think you should call him and set up an appointment to see him. Tell him I sent you."

Jack Griffin took the slip of paper and studied it.

"Listen," he said, "if you're not going to be my therapist anymore, does that mean we can see each other? Once I end it with Linda, I mean."

"No. No, it doesn't mean that. It means that we have to say goodbye. If you want me to, I'll discuss your case with Brian Ames, the psychologist I've referred you to. If you want to start fresh with him, with no input from me, then you're free to do that. This is not your problem," I repeated. "It's mine, and I'm sorry."

Jack Griffin stood up and started down the stairs. About halfway to the sidewalk, he stopped and turned.

"What a cold-hearted, man-hating bitch you are," he said. "Just like Linda. And here I thought you were different. Boy, was I wrong. I hope you go to hell."

I didn't move until he had reached his car. Then I went inside, picked up the phone, and called Michael.

"I'm a total fuckup," I said. "I am a worthless human being, and I have no excuse for staying alive."

"Someone has certainly overreacted to something," he replied. "What happened?"

"One of my neighbors was shot by a drug dealer because I set up a watch, I couldn't intervene with Kirby, who is killing himself by inches, and I had to refer my one male client to Brian Ames, my other significant ex-lover, because I forgot about the client until he was sitting on my porch and Brian's was the only telephone number I could remember."

"And you let little things like that faze you?"

"I'm afraid so."

"Taking the last one first, referring your client to Brian was probably a good move. You were in over your head with that one. However you may feel about Brian, and despite his questionable behavior with some of his graduate students, he's a reputable psychologist, and he can see this person in an institutional setting that will tend to diffuse the latent violence. And you don't need to call Brian about it unless you want to."

"I don't want to. I don't even know whether the latent violence is in the client or in me at this point."

"Fine. Then let go of the client and see how you feel. Moving to Kirby, you have to let go of him, too. You know that. Enough said. And now you have to tell me more about your neighbor getting shot."

As I told the story for the third time that day, I began to feel that maybe it wasn't totally my fault, only partially my fault.

"But still my failure," I ended. "I can't do anything

right. I'm going to call the clinic and tell them I quit and then tear up my license.''

"That's a great idea. Abandoning the women at the clinic will really make you feel better.''

"I'll only let them down sooner or later. I might as well do it now.''

"What makes you say that?''

"I gave up on my acting career, I gave up on graduate school without a doctorate, I gave up on Kirby. Are you starting to see a pattern here?''

"A distorted one,'' he answered. "I think they aren't all analogous situations. The givings-up on everything but graduate school were pragmatic decisions based on the best information available at the time, and even the doctorate was arguably a lost cause, for more reasons that Brian's erratic behavior. If you're suggesting that you can't make a commitment, I could come back with all the times you've been there for me, as a friend, over the years. Do you want to hear a few?''

"One or two might be nice.''

"The breakup with Jason was one. My sister's car accident, when I had to go to the hospital every day, was another.''

I thought about it. "I guess I ought to go to the clinic tomorrow.''

"I'm sure your clients will be glad to see you. And they will be very upset if you quit, you know that.''

I did know that.

"Every therapist has to refer a client to someone else sooner or later, you must know that, too,'' Michael added. "So much of the process depends on the personal, whatever the theory.''

"I remember that study. The biggest factor in whether patients saw therapy as a success was whether therapist and patient liked each other, not the academic bent of the therapist.''

''Graduate school was good for something. Do you like the women at the clinic?''

I didn't even have to think about it. ''Yes. I really do. I guess that means I have to go tomorrow.''

''Good. And the artist sounds like a pretty good human being, so that's something positive going on. At least he handled the situation last night well.''

''I like him, too.'' I sighed. ''Maybe I should put off ending it all for a while.''

''Maybe you should. I'd suggest we have brunch on Sunday, to continue this conversation, but you may not want to commit to that.''

''Please have brunch with me on Sunday.''

''If you insist. But I have to warn you that part of the conversation will focus on what seems to be turning into an unhealthy attraction to danger. I still don't understand why, for example, you thought you could talk to that drug dealer.''

''I'm not sure I have a good answer.'' And it was still hard for me to look at what I had done. I wouldn't have tried for anyone but Michael. ''Except to say that I think you're blowing it out of proportion. I thought I could talk to the drug dealer because I've used drugs and bought drugs and he looked harmless. And I was wrong.''

''Okay. That's healthy. More on Sunday.''

I had barely hung up when the phone rang.

''I have a couple of pieces of information for you,'' Detective Ryder said. ''First, whoever was killed in the street in front of your house wasn't a Tejeda brother. Second, we picked up Miguel Tejeda an hour ago when he showed up for his regular meeting with his parole officer. He says he isn't dealing drugs or carrying a gun and has no idea what this is about. Offered to take a lie-detector test. And he claims to have an alibi for the times of both murders. Are you willing to pick him out of a line-up?''

''Yes. Absolutely.''

I agreed to meet Ryder at the county jail in an hour. I did remember that I had a client at five, and I would be back in time to see her.

I didn't think I'd made a mistake identifying Tejeda, but it was hard to tell from the picture. If Tejeda was the baby-faced killer, he could probably beat the polygraph without breaking a sweat.

I reached the county jail ten minutes early and waited just inside the door for Ryder, who was ten minutes late.

He guided me to the staircase and down a hall to a small, dark room with a lighted stage at one end. A glass wall separated stage from audience. Ryder gestured toward a folding chair, and I sat.

Six men filed onto the stage, all wearing dark blue county jail uniforms. I was surprised at how dissimilar they looked. One had a pock-marked face, one was over forty, and two were overweight. The fifth might have looked something like Salvador—Tejeda—from two blocks away. But number six was the baby-faced monster from the night before. I knew I hadn't made a mistake.

''That one,'' I told Ryder.

''You're sure?''

''Positive.''

''Okay. We'll hold him.''

I followed Ryder out through the door, not wanting

to be left alone. But he walked to the next door and went in without me, leaving it open.

A moment later I heard a voice shouting, "She's nuts, man, this woman is nuts. I didn't kill nobody. And I got an alibi. Check it out. I'm gonna fucking sue for false arrest."

I was certain it was Salvador's voice. And I was chilled by how convincing he sounded.

I was also chilled by the thought that if the dead man wasn't one of his brothers, they were both still on the street. And they knew more or less where I lived.

Ryder found me standing where he had left me.

"Do you have a friend you can stay with for a few days?" he asked. "You might sleep better."

I shook my head. "I'm afraid Miguel Tejeda has murdered sleep. As well as my neighbor."

Ryder didn't smile. It was a cheap joke, and it didn't make a dent in my discomfort. I was sorry I'd said it.

"I may leave the lights on, though," I added. "And let a couple of people know Tejeda has been identified and arrested. I do have friends I could stay with, and I have somewhere I have to be tomorrow. But I don't like the idea of being chased out of my house. I work at home, I'm a therapist, and the idea of calling my clients and explaining why I can't see them for a while doesn't feel right."

"Okay. But for a while, whatever you do, don't do it alone at night. And think about setting up some kind of alarm, so that anyone trying to break in will wake you up." He put his hand on my shoulder, reassuring me. "I'll ask Page and Davila to drive by regularly, at least for the next night or two. A patrol car on the street tends to discourage criminal activity. I just wish we had more of them."

''Me, too. And thanks.'' I smiled honestly for the first time that day.

I liked Ryder. I considered telling him about Kirby and Gordo, but even thinking about it made me feel like Buddy the Narc.

''Listen, while I'm here, I'd like to stop by and see my client, Jorge Carrasco,'' I said.

''Your client?''

''I told you, I'm a therapist. Jorge is officially my client. His attorney added me to the visitor's list.''

Ryder laughed and took me up to the visitor's floor. The same woman was in the cage. She nodded when Ryder mentioned Jorge, and handed me a badge.

''Good luck. And be careful,'' Ryder said.

The deputy opened the barred door to let me through.

''I'll do my best.''

''Let me know if I can do anything.''

I waved a small goodbye to him and followed the guard to the same sterile room where I had met with Jorge previously. Another guard brought him in a few minutes later.

''Hey, how're you doing?'' Jorge asked, clearly pleased to see me.

''Pretty well. Although things have been a little tense. I might want to trade places with you.'' I brought him up to date on everything, including my identification of Miguel Tejeda.

''Oh, shit,'' Jorge said. ''That's too bad about Wayne. He's the one who drives the brown Honda, right?''

I nodded.

''But listen, you don't want to be in here,'' he added.

"If Miguel Tejeda is in here, you're safer out there, brothers or no brothers."

"You mean you can't even be safe in jail?"

"Trust me. You can't." He smiled. "I'm sorry. I didn't want you to get in trouble helping me."

"I know. I didn't want that, either. But it was my decision, and I'm the one responsible for it."

"You're sure?"

"I'm sure."

"Okay."

I wished I could let other people be responsible for their own decisions that easily. I would have to work on it.

The guard cleared his throat.

I didn't have anything more to say, so I stood up to leave.

"I'll be in touch."

Jorge nodded, and the guard escorted him out.

I retraced my steps behind the deputy, to the cage, to the elevator, and then down the staircase and out the front door. I hoped Jorge would be out soon. The more I knew of him, the more I liked him.

Once home, I wanted to tell Esteban what was going on, but that would have to wait until either Graciela or Ramon arrived to translate.

I didn't want to talk to Alex. I called Christopher, who agreed to act as go-between.

"Tell him I'm sorry," I said. I wondered how many times I would say I was sorry before all this was over.

"I will. He'll be glad to know the man who shot Wayne is in jail. And Faith—I'm braking a confidence telling you this, but it might help you feel better. Wayne and Alex are both HIV positive. Wayne had told Alex that he didn't want to die slowly, that when he began to deteriorate, he was going to end his life. Alex was fighting with him over it, pointing out all the new drugs and everything. Wayne was determined, though. I think he chose this.''

''Oh, hell. I don't know what to say. But thank you for telling me. If there's anything I can do for Alex, let me know.''

I felt lost and alone when I hung up.

I left the house and walked through the gazania to Marcus's kitchen door.

The stereo wasn't on, and I almost turned away. But then I heard the piano. Marcus was playing a slow, aching blues. I leaned against the door and shut my eyes, waiting for him to finish before I knocked.

''Hey, girl,'' he said.

I was glad he was dressed.

''I identified the killer,'' I said. ''The police have him in custody, but he threatened them—and by implication me—and I'm a little scared.''

He grabbed me and hugged me. ''Of course you are. What can I do?''

''Do you think you could keep the music low, just for tonight? So you could hear me if I screamed?''

''Oh, baby. You want to stay here, you can.''

''No. I don't want to be chased out of my house.''

''I will personally assign Louie to watch the street, the yard, and every access to your house. If anything happens to you, he's gone. I'll keep the music low, too, just to be on the safe side.''

''Thanks.'' I kissed his cheek without being asked.

''And don't stay there to prove how tough you are. You change your mind, you come here.''

''Thanks again.''

I disengaged myself and returned home.

I could call Richard, I knew that, or Michael, but either one might argue me into coming over, and I had meant what I said to Marcus. I didn't want to be chased out.

The two late afternoon client appointments passed without incident, and the street looked peaceful as I said goodbye to the last one.

Still, I checked to make certain that all the screens were tight and the windows locked before I went to bed that night.

Marcus kept his word, keeping the music low enough to hear me if I screamed.

Not that I screamed—there was no reason to. But I watched old movies on television almost until dawn, without a sign of trouble, and without hearing Marcus's blues, even when I went to the front of the house to check.

And his lights were on. All night.

I fell asleep at sunrise, wondering if my life would ever be sane again.

EIGHTEEN

I MADE IT TO the clinic the next morning at two minutes past ten. Elena Ortiz was sitting, waiting for me. The young woman's face brightened when I walked in the door, coffee and pastry in hand.

"I'm sorry," I said automatically. "I didn't have time to eat. Do you mind?"

"No. No problem."

Mary waved us on.

I had thought it impossible that I would be able to set aside my own problems for the day, to deal with Elena's, then Betty's, then those of my three afternoon clients. But when five o'clock arrived, I felt better than I had when I arrived.

Michael was right. I could do this.

I went home and collapsed, setting the alarm so that I could take a nap and get to Richard's house on time.

When the alarm went off at eight, I was groggy enough that I thought about cancelling. But I dragged myself up and to the bathroom for fresh makeup.

At nine o'clock, I stood on his porch, bottle of wine in hand, almost not wanting to knock. I hated dumping my problems on him, and there was no way to avoid it. I was too tired and too frightened—and too discouraged—to pretend nothing was wrong.

Richard opened the door and I walked into his arms.

He kissed me, and I considered running away from my life and hiding out with him forever. His mouth and his hands were becoming familiar, and I wanted to explore the rest of his body all over again. To hell with fear.

"First us," I whispered. "Then dinner."

"Oh, yes," he answered, paying some attention to my ear and neck in the process.

We stumbled to the bedroom, holding on.

About half an hour later, lust ebbed and fear returned. I felt I had to tell him the whole story, and that included Kirby. I wasn't certain how he would react to that. Richard was creative, fun, and easy to be with, and I didn't want to screw things up.

"What?" he asked, feeling me pull away.

"I have to tell you the rest of what's going on."

"Okay."

"I'd rather do it over dinner—in the living room."

"You want to watch tonight. That's why you wanted to make love first." He sighed, but he didn't sound surprised.

"I have to. I'll explain."

He kissed me and got up.

"I'll meet you in the kitchen."

He grabbed the jeans and sweat shirt he had dropped unceremoniously on the floor and put them back on.

I reached for my own jeans. On a less serious occasion, it would have amused me to note that we had dressed alike again. Pop psych strategy number twenty seven. If you want a man to feel comfortable, dress the way he does. Give up your identity if you have to. I would have been more concerned if I were certain what my identity had been to start with. Maybe Kirby was right. Maybe everything I did was a role, nothing was real.

Pop psych strategy number one was keep your past to yourself, except for communicable diseases. I was about to break that rule all to hell.

Richard handed me a glass of wine as I walked into the kitchen.

"Do you want to set the mat?" he asked.

"Sure."

He had placed flatware, napkins, and mat on the white tile counter. I took them into the living room and set them down near the front window.

Then I realized what I had walked past.

I was stunned by the transformation in the painting. The H O L L Y W O O D sign sparkled, the Griffith Observatory hid, the hillside houses asserted themselves unevenly. Some streets were black, some were flowing brown rivers. A spotlit sunset blasted the sky. Trees and rocks had become arrangements of atoms with darting, falling electrons.

What had started as a landscape—or so I had thought—had become L.A. in all it glory and decadence.

I dashed back to the kitchen.

"My God, how could you make love to me when I didn't even notice what you'd done?"

He turned, startled.

"I guess I got distracted. You like it?"

"Oh, dear God, yes, I love it." I started crying. "Jesus, you are brilliant."

"Hey, hey." He had been tearing salad greens. He reached out with damp hands to hold me. "That's nice. I'm glad you like it."

His face was shining like a porchlight to welcome

me home. I touched his cheek, fantasies of a return to the futon racing through my head.

A timer dinged. We backed away from each other.

"Want your fettucine al dente?" he asked.

"No other way. Drain it."

"Then go back to the living room so I can think about food."

I kissed him quickly and returned to admire the painting one more time.

Richard followed with a tray holding two plates of pasta and two bowls of salad. He had tossed the fettucine with some marinated zucchini, red and yellow peppers, and red onion, one of those Mediterranean mixtures that was mostly do-ahead and meant to be served at room temperature.

When we were both settled on the mat, he looked at me quizzically. "Well? What do you want to tell me?"

I started with the easy stuff—Miguel Tejeda, who told the cop he wasn't the guy who shot Wayne, but who had to be, and his brothers, neither of whom were Adam 103, and my fear that the violence wasn't over. I could talk about that fear. Talking about Kirby—my past with him, the events of the last week, and my fear for him now—was tougher.

"I only know Kirby McKenzie through his work," Richard said in response. "No question he's a talented actor and musician. And I've known artists like that—children of the sun. They have everything going for them, and they overreach. They fly too high, their wings melt, and they plunge into the sea."

"That's Kirby. Self-destructing as we speak. But you make it sound as if there's something glorious about it. There isn't. It's ugly."

"You're right. And this is going to sound self-serving, but I think you ought to forget about him."

"And you're right. I just don't know how to stop caring. Even if he's involved in something as ugly and stupid as murder."

"You're sure he is?"

"I'm afraid he is. And that's worse."

Richard frowned. "Even figuring that one of the Tejedas was here that night, maybe Tejeda lied about his brother meeting an Anglo. He lied about everything else. Or the Anglo could have been Kirby's friend."

"Gordo. Yes, I thought that, too."

"Now?"

I shrugged.

"What do you think you'll gain by watching tonight?" he continued.

"I don't know. I suppose I think I'm going to find out if the Tejedas are going to come after me. That's my immediate fear, that one of his brothers will try to threaten me out of the identification. But if nobody comes tonight, what do I do? Do I spend the rest of my life sitting up all night?"

"I hope not."

I laughed in spite of myself. He was taking this so well. I picked up my fork and began to eat.

"I guess I have to take it one night at a time. And by the way, the pasta is great." I had to swallow before saying more. "And I guess I have to think about moving, as much as I've resisted doing that."

Conversation lagged while we finished eating.

Richard left me alone at the window while he cleaned up the dishes and made coffee, refusing help.

"How late do you need to watch?" he asked when he returned with two mugs of latte.

"I don't know. Maybe one or two. Until I start to feel secure, or exhausted, whichever comes first."

What came first was the gray car that had blocked my path two nights earlier, cruising slowly around the corner and down the street.

"Oh, dear God," I whispered. "They're back. What am I going to do?"

"You're sure about the car?"

I nodded. "I remember the broken tail light."

"What you're not going to do is run out there," Richard said calmly. "We'll see if the car stops. If it looks like anything is going on, we'll call the police."

"If I got closer, I could get the license number. No one got the license number. If the car is registered to one of the Tejedas, that would be evidence to back up the identification, wouldn't it?"

"The car probably isn't registered to anyone. And you can't go out there."

I bristled.

The car parked in front of Alex's house, the one that used to be Wayne's as well. The lights went off. A man got out of the passenger side. He walked down a few steps and looked at the freshly painted garage doors, then up at Norman and Helena's house.

"Suppose he thinks that's where I live?" I whispered. "Norman and Helena don't have anything to do with this, they didn't even volunteer for anything. Where's the phone?"

Richard handed me a cordless receiver, and I punched in Norman's number. The machine answered on the first ring.

"Norman, pick up, it's Faith." I kept whispering as if the man in the street might be able to hear. I held on until the machine cut me off.

The man got back into the car.

Still with no lights, the car pulled away from the curb, rolled to the far end of the block, turned and came back almost to Richard's driveway. The car parked again.

"It doesn't look as if you're a target, or at least not right now." Richard was whispering, too.

"Maybe they think I live in Norman's house, and I'm not home, and they're waiting for me."

"Then why did they come to this end of the block?"

"I don't know. I don't know why any of this."

But then I did know. A dark green Jaguar convertible appeared up the block to the right.

"God, no. It's Kirby."

Kirby parked the Jaguar and walked over to the streetlight near the jacaranda tree. The man from the passenger side of the gray car walked over to meet him.

Richard grabbed the phone and hit 911.

"Operator there is a drug transaction happening under my window," he said. He gave the address. "Yes, I'm certain. The seller has been here before, and the local officers, Page and Davila, know about this. Get them out here. The seller is driving an old gray Toyota with a damaged right tail light. The buyer is one Kirby McKenzie, driving a dark green Jaguar convertible, license number—"

Richard paused and looked at me.

"4ASONG," I said.

"4ASONG. We have reason to believe he's driving under the influence of alcohol and cocaine," Richard finished.

I didn't say anything. He was right. This late at night, Kirby had to be under the influence of something.

And I felt like Buddy the Narc.

Something was happening under the streetlight. Kirby was backing toward the car, slipping something in his pocket. His other hand was low, but I caught the glint of metal.

"Kirby has a gun," I whispered.

"There are drawn guns down there," Richard snapped into the phone. "If the police don't get here quickly, someone's going to be killed."

I was out the door before Richard could put the phone down and stop me.

"Kirby, you asshole, what the fuck are you doing?" I wailed as I ran down the stairs.

Kirby looked around wildly, waving the gun. He fired it at something. In response, I heard the same cork-popping sounds I had heard two nights before. Kirby staggered, then turned and ran for his car.

"Don't," I cried. "Stop. Please. Wait."

I heard another pop and a thunk in the tree next to me. The man who had been talking to Kirby was back in the gray car. Both engines started.

And I heard a third engine behind me.

The Jaguar peeled away from the curb in a u-turn and headed up the street, the gray Toyota behind it. Richard was on the Harley, in the street next to me. I grabbed his shoulder so hard that he almost dropped the bike, but he steadied, and I threw my leg over and climbed on behind him.

The Jag ran two red lights to reach the freeway entrance, with the Toyota and the Harley following. If Kirby could get out of the city, there was no doubt that he could outrun pursuit. But he had to go through Hollywood first.

He cut across three lanes of traffic before he reached Vermon, but then he had to slow down, with traffic in the fast lane running almost bumper to bumper at seventy, and a small truck doing sixty right in front of him.

The Toyota started to follow him across, but didn't make it. Its left rear fender caught the right front fender of a speeding Chevy. Both cars spun out of control. I could hear brakes screaming, metal crumpling.

Richard kept the Harley almost on the right shoulder until we passed the spinning Toyota, then moved to the second lane. He accelerated so quickly that I had to wrap my hands in his sweat shirt, and I couldn't look back to see whether the crash behind us was the Toyota hitting someone or someone hitting the Chevy.

Bikers wear leather and goggles for good reason. This was a mild, end-of-May evening, temperature in the high sixties, but at ninety miles an hour, the windchill factor brought it down to something that felt like thirty-two degrees. Not only could I not look back to see what had happened to the Toyota, I couldn't even look ahead. My eyelids couldn't function. I could feel my face starting to ripple with cold. My sweat shirt and jeans disappeared, my flesh was blown away, I was nothing but bones sticking to Richard's back, with the wind sneaking in at my joints, tearing through the marrow of my bones, and bursting forth again.

I caught a glimpse of the Highland exit sign through slit eyelids as we slowed down. Caltrans had closed two lanes for maintenance work. The Jaguar was one lane over and maybe a quarter of a mile ahead, but Richard threaded the narrow space between a Jeep and a minivan, still at sixty, to catch up with him. Kirby had the advantage when a lane was open, but Richard could split lanes when Kirby was boxed in. As Kirby neared the end of the highway project, Richard and I were right behind.

Kirby accelerated to the right, knocking over three of the orange rubber cones that had blocked the lane from traffic. Before Richard could follow, the Jaguar was back in front of us, but several cars ahead. Kirby veered left to avoid the backup at the Universal Studios exit, narrowly missing a red Ford, but Richard had anticipated the move and zipped between two cars to reach the fast lane.

We were nearing the junction of the Hollywood and Ventura Freeways. Kirby was staying on the Hollywood, which would take him through North Hollywood, across the tip of Van Nuys, then to the Golden State Freeway. From there it was clear driving to Santa Clarita and points north. If he couldn't be stopped soon, Richard would lose him.

The terror of high speeds on a motorcycle comes from the forced awareness of your own vulnerability, your own mortality. The steel juggernauts rumbling along on either side are waiting for one slip of balance, of judgment, to toss you whirling into the night sky and crush you beneath their ruthless wheels when you come crashing down. I wanted to be part of Richard's body, part of his mind, anything but a dead weight behind him. My sight disappeared again in the swirl of wind beneath my eyelids, my bones froze and crackled and threatened to shatter as we raced along in the darkness.

Something happened. We began to slow down. I fought to control my eyelids and saw the Jaguar weaving in front of us. It slued to the right, trying to make the Sherman Way exit, the sign a floating blur against the night sky, but it rolled to a stop on the shoulder a few feet beyond.

Richard pulled up next to the car.

Kirby was slumped over the steering wheel.

I tried to call out his name, but nothing was working. My muscles shook, my teeth chattered, and what was supposed to be my voluntary nervous system tried to shut down. I wouldn't let it. I dragged my leg over the bike and stumbled to the door of the Jag.

I jerked the door open and fell on top of him. His coat was warm and sticky, but his face was cold. I couldn't get his name out.

His head fell over in my arms, and his eyes opened. He tried to smile.

"In the movie," he whispered. "Taking human life was so easy. And then I did it—by accident, really. He threatened me with his knife, and it was just like in the movie, so easy. I took it and killed him with it. I thought I could do it again, so easy, just like the movie."

His body shuddered and jerked, but he smiled, he kept smiling, even as his eyes lost their focus.

"So easy," he whispered.

I tried again to say his name, I wanted to say his name, I wanted something to come out of my mouth.

Then I started screaming.

NINETEEN

"YOU'VE HANDLED THIS awfully well, all things considered," Michael said.

"That only means I'm not suicidal and so far I've kept the rest of my clients. I suppose that's well. Would you mind getting Tony's attention so that I can have another latte?"

Michael raised his head and Tony, the waiter, was there in an instant to take my order for a second latte. I would have asked for more water, too, but he was gone without looking at me.

We were brunching again at the same small cafe on Santa Monica Boulevard, with the black umbrellas on the tables too close to the street. Breathing exhaust fumes was the price I was paying for Michael's friendship with Tony.

"And you're thinking about moving, and you're willing to give the relationship with Richard some time. Those are both good," Michael said.

"And none of that solves my crisis of conscience. Maybe becoming a therapist was just an excuse to interfere with other people's lives," I moaned. "Maybe it's all a kind of internal performance, just another role."

"Well, if that's true, and you're aware of it, you can still be a good therapist. Play a role at work—lots of people do. Just play it well. Play the role of the world's best therapist. Then be someone else the rest of the time if you want. Nobody ever said your work had to be your whole life. I know it tends to become that for actors, and I can see why you had an identity crisis when you left television.''

''That happens to everybody,'' I said firmly. ''Who you are is who you see when you look at yourself in the studio monitor. The public person is who all the people you meet relate to. You become the public person, and there is no private person. When there is no longer a public person, there is no longer a you. I became a student, and I became a therapist, and I'm still not certain who the private person is.'' I crossed my arms and hunched down in my chair.

''Then make her up as you go along. Improvise. Has this finished your involvement with Jorge Carrasco?''

''More or less. I'll go to the preliminary hearing tomorrow, as planned. Miriam Stern thinks my testimony will be enough to get the judge to drop the murder charge. She hopes the assault charge will go away, too.''

''What about Adam 103?''

''Unknown forever, unless someone comes forward to claim the body, and that doesn't seem likely.''

Tony arrived with my latte. I grabbed it out of his hand and took a sip.

''What could I have done differently?'' I asked.

''Probably nothing. Or you would have,'' Michael answered. ''The same with Kirby. He did what he did.''

''But he didn't really mean to. He was desperate and in debt. And he didn't ask Evan and Dixie for help, which still puzzles me.''

"Faith, he would have had to admit his addiction—to someone besides Gordo—discuss his addiction with his parents—to do that. Not even Dixie could have denied it then. Are you sure he committed murder by accident?"

I nodded. "I think so. They were his dying words, after all, and I don't think he'd lie to me as he was dying." I rushed on, not wanting to linger over that. I knew I had some grief to deal with. I wasn't certain how much. "I'm guessing a lot, but here's what I think happened that night. The Tejedas were dealing from their usual spot on the corner. Kirby saw the anonymous kid, the thief in my jacket, buy drugs with the money he got from selling my stereo and jewelry. Kirby needed the coke. He needed it so much that he decided he deserved it, that it didn't matter how he got it."

"Be careful—don't try to justify what he did."

I shook my head. "I'm not. I'm just trying to understand it. Kirby had played so many tough guys on screen that he was sure he could do it in life. And the kid was small, looked like an easy mark. So the actor in him took over. But the kid pulled a knife. Kirby panicked, had enough martial arts training to take it away from him, and stabbed him with it. He picked up the cocaine and walked calmly into Marcus's house."

"How could he go out to look at the body later?"

"Acting skills, ultimate cool, and good dope."

Michael used the last little bit of English muffin to sop up the hollandaise sauce from his eggs florentine.

"Nobody ever said Kirby lacked talent," he said.

"Just amazing, isn't it, the ways talented people find to screw themselves up."

"And self-deprecation is one of the worst. Along with self-pity."

"You can't deny I made things worse."

"Yes, I can. The Tejeda brothers are in jail and Jorge is getting out. That's better. And you aren't responsible for either Wayne's death or Kirby's."

"Richard said the same thing."

"For an artist and a madman, he's pretty smart."

"Richard isn't a madman," I said. "A lot of artists are a little crazy, Richard included, but he isn't a madman. The wild motorcycle chase happened because he knew I needed to be there at the end, and he was right. It was the only way I could be free to give my relationship with him a chance."

"I'm truly glad you want it to have a chance."

"I think so. Early sex is a highly overrated road to intimacy, though. I need to back off and think about it."

"Good. And you can still see him after you move. You'll just have to drive instead of walk."

I shut my eyes, grateful for the warm afternoon sun. "I know you're right. I wish I knew where to go."

"In the meantime, while you're thinking, would you like three days in Maui? Pretty Kitty is filming Elizabeth's next commercial there, and they've given me two first class plane tickets and a suite. I know Elizabeth would like to have you along."

"You don't want to take Tony?" The remark sounded catty enough to have come from Elizabeth, and I wanted to call it back.

"Elizabeth hasn't met him," Michael said calmly, "and I don't want to do anything that might make her uncomfortable while she's working."

"When do we leave?"

"A week from Tuesday."

"You're on. And thank you."

I finished my latte, fought Michael in vain for the check, and left him alone at the table, ordering his third latte.

I drove the few miles home wondering what I was going to do when I got there.

Graciela was waiting on the porch, holding a huge basket of fruit wrapped in yellow cellophane topped with a sparkling yellow bow.

"Here," she said. "For you. Nino, Jorge's boss, put it together. We're all grateful for what you did."

"This is wonderful. Thank you. And thank Nino. But Jorge isn't out yet." I took the basket from Graciela's outstretched arms.

"No, but you can do it. After this, the judge will have to listen to you, even if he won't listen to the girl."

"Miriam Stern will get him out. Not me."

"Maybe she'll get him out. Not without you. You're the best captain of the block we could have had."

"Thank you."

I held out my hand and Graciela awkwardly shook it. I watched her walk down the stairs.

Marcus's kitchen door flew open, letting out a blast of sound.

"Hey, girl," he called, leaning around the doorpost. "I hear the dealers are in jail and the streets are safe again. And the homeboy will most likely be out of jail. You did good."

"Do you really think so?"

"I do."

"And Kirby?"

"He did it to himself, girl, he did it to himself. There's a memorial service on Wednesday. You going?"

I thought about Kirby, thought about Dixie. I had already said goodbye to Kirby, and Dixie wouldn't want to see me.

"No. No, I don't think so."

"Turn down that stereo!" Norman shouted from his kitchen window.

"See you later," Marcus said, pulling his door shut.

Amy rubbed against my leg.

"Come on in," I told her. "Although you have food, you know that."

I balanced the basket and opened the door. Amy and Mac raced in ahead. I could tell them later that they were facing three days in a cage with the vet while I went to Maui. Normally I would have left them at home, asking Louie to feed them, but this time, to insure my rest and recreation, they had to be boarded.

A note that had been tucked against the jamb fell to the carpet. I picked it up.

"My lease is up in two months. The beach or the mountains? Love, Richard."

If that was an offer, it wasn't my answer. Whatever was going on between us, I couldn't move in with him. At least not yet.

The beach or the mountains. Or neither.

I had time. I'd think about it when I was ready.

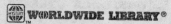

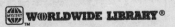

Take 2 books and a surprise gift FREE!

SPECIAL LIMITED-TIME OFFER

Lost in Austin

A Tony Kozol Mystery

When a broken arm sidelines the guitarist for a popular country band, struggling musician Tony Kozol gets a gig as the temporary replacement. But when the band arrives in Austin for a week at the Southwest Music Conference—murder takes center stage.

The victim was a roadie with the group, and Tony soon spots an unsettling connection to the band—especially when the body of a pretty young groupie is found next. Sounds to Tony like a song in the making: a tale full of heartbreak and woe, longing and desire. It could be a hit. That is, if he lives long enough to write it.

J. R. Ripley

"J. R. Ripley continues to delight."
—*Midwest Book Review*

Available April 2002
at your favorite retail outlet.

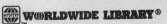